OWNING

WEDNESDAY

Annabel Joseph

Scarlet Rose Press
Atlanta, Georgia

To Audrey and Doris,
My first readers.

CHAPTER ONE

Wednesday shifted next to her Master, trying not to stare at the man across the table. Vincent had introduced him as Daniel Laurent, one of his former art students and now a successful movie-set designer. Wednesday was a little starstruck.

And a lot aroused.

She didn't know why this friend of Vincent's affected her so strongly. She was quite content with her handsome, dark-eyed Master. Content was not a strong enough word—she worshipped him. Vincent was in his early fifties, stern and intelligent. Daniel was closer to her age, perhaps thirty, and blond in contrast to Vincent's dark coloring. His personality was a contrast too, laid-back and open. He smiled a lot. God, that smile. So easy and charming. So easy to get lost in...

You have a master, Wednesday. And he's not blond.

This dinner outing was a birthday present of sorts from Vincent, who rarely took her on dates, much less introduced her to friends—unless he meant to share her with them. Wednesday knew she would be serving Daniel later, but even so, she wasn't getting the usual "you're gonna be my bitch" vibe. Daniel just looked at her like she was a normal woman, and treated her with friendly respect. She supposed, in general, she did look totally normal. Vincent collared and cuffed her often in private but never in public, so there was nothing to make anyone look at her sideways or realize she was kinky. She did have striking coloring—thick, curly black hair and light blue eyes lined with black lashes that contrasted sharply with her pale skin.

Daniel had light blue eyes too, but his scruffy blond hair seemed much more appropriate to their shade. His gaze caught hers on more than one occasion, and she began to hope that he found her attractive. Her lips were painted, as usual, a deep, rich plum that her Master preferred. She knew she had full, pretty lips and a nice smile. Vincent loved her mouth, in more ways than one. What did Daniel think of her mouth? She imagined opening her lips wide and moaning around his cock, and a guilty flush of arousal warmed her cheeks. She tried to put the brakes on her libido, wary of angering her Master. She glanced at Vincent, and he frowned back at her. Too late.

What Daniel thought of all this, she had no idea. She watched his body language, trying to glean what he might be like in their scene later. God, he was so handsome. Usually she put up with third partners, whether male or female, because Vincent wanted her to. For the first time, she was excited herself.

Daniel and her Master fought over the check—Daniel won—and then they set out for Vincent's house. Daniel said he would drive separately, so Vincent and Wednesday endured a tense drive alone in his car through the city. Wednesday liked Vincent's house. It was neat and tastefully decorated, and bright with light for his painting and sculpting. Vincent's home was utterly perfect, like him. It was impossible to misbehave in such an austere space.

During the drive, Wednesday waited for Vincent to clue her in on how he felt about the fact that she was lusting after his friend. Unfortunately, he gave her nothing, only the equivocal silence she knew so well.

So she sat, silent and anxious, and waited to see how things would go. She hoped he wouldn't be too hard on her, since she'd tried, at least, to hide her attraction.

Inside, Vincent offered him a drink, which Daniel refused, to her relief. Not that she imagined him as the type to get drunk and sloppy when he played. She just didn't want to wait for things to get going. Vincent led him to the playroom, which looked like the rest of the house, only the walls were soundproof and there were hooks hidden everywhere and cabinets full of toys. Toys that Wednesday knew, by this point, exceedingly well. Toys that Daniel, having been invited here, was surely familiar with too.

There was no real talk, no negotiating. Vincent told her to undress, and she complied. No sexy striptease—Vincent wouldn't like it. She took off her shoes and dress and set them in a neat pile. But as she began to unhook her stockings, Daniel said, "Have her leave them on."

She looked at Vincent, who nodded shortly. She went to her Master and knelt while he buckled on her collar and cuffs. He asked Daniel, "What do you want?"

Daniel looked back at him and then at her. "I'd like to have her alone."

"No, I don't think so," said Vincent with a terse smile. "But she's perfectly capable of attending to us both." He made a subtle gesture in Daniel's direction.

She crawled to Daniel in her stockings and heels and knelt at his feet with her lips parted just slightly. She watched for any directions. Daniel gazed down at her for a long moment, and she wasn't sure what was going on behind those piercing blue eyes. Then he reached down and tipped her head back.

"Nice," he said finally. "You can suck me. Help me undress." He undid his pants while she worked on his shoes and socks. He had his shirt off before she could even get to it. He seemed eager to show her his body, and no wonder, because nude, he was absolutely breathtaking. Golden California tan, muscles that looked strong and prominent, but not too prominent. Broad shoulders tapered to a blond-furred chest and cut abs that ended in... Wow. She wanted to caress him, to run her hands all over his perfectly honed body to feel every hard and sinuous part of him, but she didn't. She only waited for him to roll on a condom and guide his cock into her mouth.

Daniel was a big man, but so was Vincent, so she had no problems accommodating his size. She threw herself into her service with perhaps a bit too much abandoned devotion. She opened wide, licking the underside of his cock, then brushing tiny tongue strokes around the swollen head. He wasn't gentle and found the back of her throat quickly, grasping her shoulders. Rather than alarming her, the rough usage elicited an even deeper submission. She used her lips and tongue to pleasure him, moaning softly, closing her eyes to concentrate on the sensation of being taken so decisively by a man she'd just met. He smelled different, a new musk. He had a different rhythm, a different thrust than Vincent. He had novel contours, and those fingers digging into her shoulders...

She sighed against the satiny hardness of his cock, wanting more. She reached out to touch him, alert to any signals of rejection. Sometimes Vincent pushed her hands away and only let her use her mouth. But Daniel slid a hand down her back with an encouraging groan.

"Oh yes. Touch me. Play with my balls, girl."

She skimmed her fingertips over his crisp hair and his firm, pendulous sac. She slid her hands up to grip his rod and licked around the base, then down to tease his balls. She could feel his body tighten in response—feel it in his thighs and the fingers that twisted in her hair. He pulled her head back and made a low noise. She opened her mouth wide in response, his willing, waiting receptacle.

Again, he slid deep, and she fought not to gag. She sucked him in a faster rhythm, using her hands in any way she thought might please him. She stroked his balls and massaged his shaft, and was rewarded with a hiss from between his teeth.

"Yes, more. Don't stop."

His voice was a demanding, low rumble. He tightened his hands in her hair, and her pussy clenched from the sensation of being controlled, used. God, she was so hot she wanted to hump against his leg. Her whole body hummed at the same compelling pitch as his words. Was it only attraction that had her so excited? She made a fist and pressed it against her thigh. She wanted to touch herself, rub herself into oblivion, but she didn't dare.

This is not about you.

She made a soft sound, a small moan of capitulation, and went back to working his cock, kissing, sucking, licking. She sensed him nearing his climax. She felt flushed and frantic to bring him to that peak of completion. This first encounter was like a fire burning too hot and bright, and it imprinted everything about him on her like sharp little burns from ashes: the fresh-spicy smell of him, the tug of his fingers in her hair, the width of his cock between her lips.

He came with a groan and a sweet tremor that she felt beneath her fingertips. After a moment, she released his cock with a long, wanton slide of tongue over latex. She furtively swiped a hand over her lips and chin. She'd drooled on him like a messy whore.

What now? Her brain was fuck-fuzzy. At a snap of Vincent's fingers, she was scurrying over to him, rolling on his condom, and throwing herself into orally serving him.

But she was ashamed that even as she knelt before Vincent, thoughts of Daniel crept into her mind. She tried to push them away and center on serving her Master. She licked and sucked him, using her tongue to tease his balls in the same way she'd pleasured Daniel. She could feel his rigid stance and tried even harder to please him, taking him deep in her throat for long minutes while he fucked her without tenderness. She gagged, and her eyes watered. The encounter felt angry and uncomfortable, but she groveled before him anyway, giving herself up for his use. It felt like penance. Atonement.

She wondered if Daniel was watching her, and what he was thinking. *Focus. Focus on your Master, stupid girl.* How many times had Vincent beaten that rule into her in the early days of her training? Vincent twisted his fingers in her hair, and he made some sound, a short comment to Daniel. Then she felt warm thighs against the backs of her thighs and Daniel's hands around her waist.

She didn't stop what she was doing. She still serviced her Master, but she felt strangely split, the greater part of her attention on the new man behind her. She'd been fucked like this many times, and given no thought to the third partner's existence beyond a slave's attention to duty. Now her body burned with a heightened arousal. Daniel moved his hands from her waist to the back of her ass, then down to nudge her thighs wider. His fingers were firm against her skin, and the matter-of-fact way he manipulated her made her pussy ache to be filled. Filled by him.

Please...

He tightened his hands, and that hard, beautiful cock she'd been dreaming of pushed inside, spreading her, forcing her open with an exquisite solidity. She arched to take all of him. He pressed his hips against her ass as he seated himself to the hilt and stayed there, as if he wanted to be sure she focused on his total possession of her. She made a wild sound around the barrier of Vincent's cock, and Daniel responded in kind.

He began to move, fucking her fast and deep. His balls banged against her clit, a rhythmic tease of sensation. She wiggled her hips, trying to feel more of the delicious contact. Her pelvis ached, and she felt an alarming rush of heat to her thighs and the tips of her nipples. The way he fucked her—so rough, yet so controlled. She was grounded by his steady grip on her hips, and still she had the feeling she might lose herself completely at any moment.

She had to fight the impulse to turn away from Vincent and reach behind her to scratch those thighs, to draw him closer. She wanted to collapse on the floor and grind back against him, doing whatever she had to do to satisfy the need in her clit. Daniel braced her upright, preventing such an ignominious breach of conduct with one arm tight around her waist. *Careful, careful.* Vincent owned her orgasms, and Wednesday was not permitted to come without permission. She tried to focus, tried not to drift away on her own pleasure and forget her place.

Wednesday refocused her efforts on worshipping her Master's cock. She took him deep, making the small, frantic lust noises she knew aroused him. His cock jerked in her mouth, an acknowledgment of her efforts. Just as she regained her concentration, Daniel reached around to pinch and toy with her nipples. He swirled a deft fingertip around each peak, a soft, excruciating taunt, then pinched and tugged until she whimpered. She pushed back against his cock, her animal sounds muffled by Vincent's thrusting. The hot teasing and torment goaded her to a frightening apex.

She put her hands on Vincent's thighs to center herself, one last grasp at regaining her quickly ebbing control. She knew Vincent wouldn't grant her permission to come, not this early in the scene, and she would not disgrace him by begging. Instead, she gave herself up to the feeling of being used, being conquered by both men.

She jerked her hips each time Daniel thrust in her, and her moaning became a steady vibration against her Master's cock in her mouth and throat. Daniel moved closer behind her. He trailed his fingers down her front to rest at the top of her cleft for just a moment before slipping lower, straight to her throbbing clit. *Oh my God.* He slid his fingers over it with devastating dexterity as he continued to ram her with his cock.

The pleasure was unbearable, piercing and electric. With a backward jerk of her hips and a soft gasp against Vincent's cock, she toppled over the precipice and climaxed despite all her efforts at control. Orgasmic shocks squeezed her pelvis and shot up to her throbbing nipples. She rode it out in secret, shamed silence, never stopping her attentions to Vincent. Daniel braced her more tightly as she nearly collapsed forward. Then he pulled away.

Wednesday threw herself into pleasuring Vincent, guilty recriminations pounding in her head. *You lost control. You came without your Master's permission.* The worst thing was, she hadn't even been thinking of serving Vincent at the time. She'd only been thinking of Daniel and the way he was stroking her clit and pounding her pussy. She'd been preoccupied, reeling from his hands and their magic touch. After Vincent was done with her mouth, Wednesday stayed on her hands and knees with her head down, not even able to look at her Master's face.

"Finish," he said gruffly.

Wednesday peeled off Vincent's condom and crawled over to dispose of it in the trash.

"Very nice," Daniel said, sounding bemused. "Full service. By the way, your submissive came while I was fucking her."

Wednesday grimaced as she returned to the two men, but Vincent looked unsurprised. "Sometimes she's a real slut that way. I'll punish her. Or you may, if you wish."

Wednesday could tell just by Vincent's tone that he was furious. So be it. What was done was done. Daniel had made her come, and now he'd be the one to punish her for it. She was dying to know the strength of his hand. Vincent rattled off the implements at his disposal, asking Daniel which he wanted to use.

"I want to spank her over my lap," Daniel said, "if you don't mind."

"No, I don't mind. Why don't you plug her while you're at it, and we can both take a turn in her ass when you're finished?"

"Sure. That sounds good. Come, Wednesday." Daniel patted his lap. Even in her disgrace, it thrilled her to hear her name on his lips, in the authoritative, quiet way he said it. She crawled over, and he pulled her across his thighs. He took a moment to run his hand over her ass, then traced down the straps of her garter belt to where they met the lacy tops of her stockings. She was perfectly in position, but he manhandled her anyway, arranging her hips closer to his and then taking her arm firmly.

"I could restrain her with the cuffs if you like," Vincent said.

"No, thanks." Daniel laughed, pinching just at the underside of her ass cheek. "I think I can handle this one." Her tender skin throbbed where he'd pinched her, and he was so strong, so solid. It was so much more apparent now that she was held over his lap. She looked up to see Vincent handing him a toy for her ass. God, he'd chosen a huge one. Daniel was careful, but still she moaned in soft complaint as he drove it home.

"Hush," he said. "You know it doesn't hurt that much."

Then he began to spank her, even giving her a short warm-up first. God, this man was wonderful, she thought, but she quickly realized why the warm-up was necessary with him. He progressed from light smacks to spanking like a pile driver—hard and direct, relentless and fast. The pain took her breath away.

There was no time to rest and collect herself between blows. The stinging, punishing smacks fell without respite, without any downtime. It was so difficult to process the pain that she couldn't even daydream anymore about how much he turned her on. It was probably for the best, since she wasn't meant to enjoy this. Punishment, not play.

She grasped Daniel's leg, trying to work through the building pain, then let go, making a fist. She didn't dare reach back and try to shield herself, but at last she had to cry out and beg for mercy.

"Please...please, Sir!"

"Be a good girl, Wednesday," he said in a patient voice. "I'll stop when you've had enough."

He did eventually stop when she'd had enough...well, perhaps a bit too much. Her ass was on fire as he caressed the hot globes with teasing fingertips. She hadn't cried, not really. Well, almost. Maybe a few silent tears of frustration squeezed from her tightly closed eyes, but now she opened them and wiggled her bottom under his hand. She rubbed her hip against his cock, and he chuckled when she swallowed and went still.

"She takes a good spanking, Vincent."

"She takes a good strapping and cropping too. Paddling. She's an obedient girl most of the time. Hold her, and I'll cane her a little. She hates the cane."

Holy shit. Vincent was really mad. Daniel released her and pushed her off his lap. Wednesday slumped onto the floor, her insides turning to mush. Canings were hard to take, except for the welcome catharsis that followed. She didn't want her Master to stay so mad.

She turned on her knees and offered her hands to Daniel, but instead he drew her closer and had her lay her head in his lap. She folded her hands at the back of her neck, and he held them there for her—his cool, firm hands closed around her clenched ones.

Vincent laid into her, ten hard stripes. Each stroke whistled down and contacted her ass in a line of liquid, torturous fire, and each time she jerked and cried out pitifully against Daniel's thighs. Even Daniel's scent and heat couldn't distract her from the torment. Even his hands, his unforgiving hold on her couldn't fully shelter her from the frustration Vincent was venting on her already red-hot ass. The spanking Daniel had given her had been painful but playful. Vincent's caning really hurt, most of all because it was fueled by anger. By the end she was a complete mess, bawling and straining against Daniel's grip.

"God, Vincent," he said. "She's a beautiful girl."

Vincent didn't answer. Wednesday nestled her tear-dampened cheek in Daniel's lap for a moment, then kissed and nibbled softly, just once, at the juncture of Daniel's hard thigh. It was a forward, naughty thing to do, but she did it anyway. He shifted, and she heard the rattle of a condom again. Daniel guided his sheathed cock to her lips.

He rubbed and caressed her shoulders as she served him. This time he sat still while she held him and sucked him at her own pace. He was steel-hard, thick, and warm in her mouth. This second blowjob felt like leisurely enjoyment compared to the intensity of the one before. Vincent pulled the toy from her ass, and she braced at the piercing pain of her sphincter stretching, aching. He thrust in her hard, before the ache had fully subsided. Her Master held her hips and fucked her while Daniel slid in and out of her mouth. She was powerless and hurt, used and objectified, and all of it excited her. She felt at that moment absolutely mastered, lost and bodiless and fully given over to sex, to her Master.

Her Masters.

The Master at her front, filling her mouth and stroking her hair, and the Master at her back who plumbed her secret, vulnerable place without quarter. Vincent didn't hurt her, with the toy and lube already easing the way—he just shamed her and put her in her place.

Daniel's cock pacified her, and she gripped his length as a lifeline. Slow, smoldering need burned in her empty pussy, in her nipples as she rubbed them against the crisp hair of Daniel's thighs. The cane stripes burned on her ass as Vincent pinched and squeezed them. Soon his thrusts quickened, and he gripped her hips hard. He came with a jerk and a grunt.

Daniel, already hard and ready from her oral attentions, took his turn next. He knelt behind her and spread her cheeks wide, then slid in balls-deep. She shuddered, the leashed sexual tension within her shaken loose by his closeness, his eager, proprietary use of her body. She was Vincent's, but Daniel made her his so effortlessly.

Somehow she knew this act would conclude their scene and that she would never see Daniel again, so she gave herself up completely to the painful-sweet sensation, to the invasion of his body in hers. His hard, thick cock, in and out, deep inside, then back, then deep again with a conquering burn. With this act, he had taken up residence in every one of her holes—mouth, pussy, ass.

He pressed and touched all over her, urging her higher and higher. Her pussy throbbed, aching for release. He grabbed her mons and slid a finger between the slick lips of her sex, then started tapping her clit in a steady rhythm. The focused stimulation was too much—he was torturing her. Her pussy flared each time he touched her clit, and his ass-pounding strokes were pushing her closer and closer to orgasm. When she drew up taut, determined not to come without permission again, he leaned close to her, right next to her ear, and whispered, "Go ahead, come."

Seconds later she came hard and long, but she didn't make a sound or any outward sign. All the arousal from her center broke wide, drowning her, and her ass clamped down on the hot fullness of his cock. The secrecy of it seemed to intensify her climax. Daniel came after her, pounding against her, and she let out a soft moan under cover of his cry. He fell over her, breathless, and nipped the back of her neck, just as she'd nipped his thigh. As if he was telling her, *It will be our secret.*

Or maybe *Remember me* was what he'd actually meant.

As if she could she ever forget him. Thanks to him, she'd lapsed hopelessly from how she'd been trained. She'd felt too much, wanted too much, lusted too much, lost control of herself. She stayed where she was, trying to collect herself. After Daniel pulled away, Vincent yanked her up by her collar.

"Wednesday, thank our guest."

She murmured quick, breathless thanks to the floor at Daniel's feet. Then Vincent dragged her to the corner and hooked her cuffs to a bolt in the wall. She hung her head and laid her hot forehead against the wall's cool surface. He and Daniel talked for a few more moments, perhaps even a quarter hour, about professional matters: each other's art, upcoming plans. Vincent gave no suggestion of a future meeting, and Daniel eventually bid him good-bye. She wondered if he'd looked over at her one last time before he left.

If he had, he would have seen a pitiful creature, beaten, tethered, with her head bowed. A guilty girl bracing, resigned, for more pain. She had wild visions of Daniel rescuing her, whisking her away like some romantic hero. *She's mine now. Only I can hurt her, not you.* Silly visions. She was tearful, but also buzzing with the strange euphoria Daniel had triggered within her. She was so confused.

Vincent returned and sat across the room for a long while in utter silence. The only sound was her shallow breathing and her heartbeat pounding in her ears. It was punishment enough, his deep disapproval washing over her in waves. He finally walked over and stood right behind her.

"You're a little slut, you know."

She let out a sob.

"Tears? Save it. Are you thinking of him now?"

"I'm sorry, Master," she said in a voice that sounded like a plea.

"I'm sorry too. I didn't ask him here for your pleasure. I asked him here to use you like the sex toy you are. And he did, although he seemed to think you belong to him now. Who do you belong to, Wednesday?"

"I belong to you, Master. Only you!"

"Do you?" He said the words quietly, but he might as well have screamed them.

"Yes, Master. Yes!" She gathered the courage to turn and look at him. "Please, Master, I belong only to you."

"Turn back around. I know you do."

He left her and came back with a whippy crop. He used it to mark her buttocks, her legs and her back, and while she moved from him a little when the biting blows fell, she mostly stood and took them. She let him beat her, because she felt she deserved punishment. She needed expiation. By the time he finished with the crop, she ached. She hurt. When he released her cuffs, she stumbled and almost fell forward. He yanked her up again, and it scared her that still, still he seemed angry.

"Happy birthday, Wednesday," he said tightly as he unhooked her collar and cuffs. He dragged her upstairs and sent her to sleep in another room for the night. She wanted to die. She wanted to plead for forgiveness. She wanted to return to before she'd laid eyes on Daniel. But there was no way to go back.

2 CHAPTER TWO

Daniel needed a damn map. It had been some years since he'd navigated the hallowed halls of UCLA's Fine Arts building. He turned a corner, then another. Fuck, he had to backtrack. He was completely lost.

He'd been feeling lost frequently of late.

He blamed Vincent, the man who had more or less summoned him to his office. Vincent had been cryptic about the reason, but Daniel had a good enough idea what—or who—he wanted to talk about. Otherwise he wouldn't be here, wandering around and feeling like a fool.

Daniel was not generally a foolish person. Playful sometimes, silly, yes, but never a fool, and certainly never over a woman, but well...people changed. He thought he'd had his head on pretty straight when he got into this life—the BDSM clubs, the meet-ups, the organized underworld where people exchanged accepted social rules for a dance of their own, a sometimes erotic, sometimes bizarre dance of power and submission. *Hurt me. Own me. Take me. Want me. Be my Master. Be my slave.*

He'd always been attracted to this dance. He could remember being nine or ten years old, chasing girls on the playground just to hold them down, just to see that spark of rebellion in their eyes and feel them struggle to get away. The best ones only pretended to struggle, looking at him as if they shared a secret. *I understand you, and you understand me.* He chased those rare girls again and again. In time he became friends with them, and by the end of his college years he'd found the D/s scene, where those girls were everywhere.

He was never completely at home in the fetish clubs, though. He thought if he stuck it out he would run into the girl he needed, who needed him and what he wanted to give. But he found the clubs were mostly posturing and falseness, the playing of roles that ended on a word.

Daniel didn't want a scene. He wanted a relationship, but it seemed everyone around him preferred finite games and empty sex. The submissives wanted you to do what they wanted, what they liked, what they preferred, and the Dominants played along, only pretending to have control.

He played along too, out of necessity, and inevitably each scene ended, and he returned, unsatisfied, to real life. He had grown discouraged and cynical, thinking that was all there could ever be to it. That was, until Vincent invited him to his house on a cold, rainy March night, and Daniel learned there was a place for deeper love in this strange world after all.

As much as sharing went on in the scene, for him, sharing Wednesday had been a first. He'd expected some brassy pseudoslut, but instead he got Wednesday Carson. Quiet, mysterious, utterly submissive. If she had balked even a little, he would have turned on his heel and left, no matter how much he ached to put his hands on her.

But she came to him with absolute trust and openness and no shame at all. At the end he'd held her lovely clenching hands and kept her still while Vincent caned her, and he'd thought, suddenly, of those secret, shared looks on the schoolyard ground. *I understand you, and you understand me. We understand each other. Your secret is mine.*

Here was the girl for him, serious and complicated, smart and beautiful. She worked as an editor at a specialty publishing company. She was obviously intelligent, but besides that, she was just perfect in every way. She was petite but not skinny, pale and delicate but not sickly, and attractive to the point he couldn't look away. She had black hair in a mass of curls falling to her shoulders, and crazy, pale blue eyes that made him want to stare.

Too bad she was already in service to another.

Damn. He could have sworn Vincent's office was in the east wing. He realized he was on the wrong floor altogether and found the stairwell. He took the steps two at a time and finally arrived at Vincent's corner office, late and slightly breathless. The door was ajar, so Daniel knocked and pushed it open. He looked around the pristine, organized space, hoping Wednesday might be there, although he was ninety-five percent sure she wouldn't be.

Vincent gave a small, almost imperceptible laugh, and Daniel flushed. Jesus, he hated the man. He was a great teacher, but he could be a nasty human being.

"She's not here. I'm sorry if that's why you came."

Daniel entered and shut the door behind him before taking the chair in front of Vincent's desk. "I came because you asked me to come. But I hope she's well." He added the last trying to make it sound offhand, like an afterthought. Vincent looked at him over his laptop with a ruthlessly dissecting gaze.

"She's fine. She seems to have survived your rousing stint as our third partner, what was it, a couple weeks ago?"

One week, three days, and about...oh, eight hours, Daniel thought. "That's great, Vincent. So what's up?"

Vincent was quiet another moment, slowly closing his laptop. "I lied. She's not exactly fine. How did you think the scene went?"

"I don't know. It's not like I've done a ton of threesomes." He shrugged. "I certainly enjoyed myself. She seemed to enjoy herself too."

Vincent steepled his fingers and leaned back in his leather chair. He curled his lip slightly. "She did. Perhaps too much. She's been...wavering in her service to me."

Daniel watched Vincent closely, but as usual the older man cloaked any deeper emotions he might be feeling. Daniel was left to connect his own dots, and he felt a sudden, selfish hope. He stayed silent, knowing any words he uttered might give away his excitement at Vincent's news.

Vincent stared over Daniel's shoulder. He leaned forward on his elbows, rubbing his forehead. He looked old, his true age, for the first time Daniel could recall.

"I want you to take over with Wednesday."

Daniel broke into a fit of surprised coughing. "I'm sorry. You want me to—what?"

"Be with Wednesday. I want you and her to be together. I want her to have a life, a life she can't have with me."

Daniel sat there, stunned.

Vincent sighed heavily at his silence. "I've been with her for five years, and I'm the only one who's been with her. She's never had any other relationships."

God, really? The only one?

"I need to let go of her, but I can't let go. Not unless..."

"Unless what?"

"Unless I know she'll be okay. She came to me a baby, an innocent. I feel...protective of her." He paused, staring off again. He compressed his lips in a tight line. "She's very special to me."

Daniel watched him, watched the internal struggle. "If she's so special to you, why don't you try to make things work? Why pass her off? How does she feel about this?"

"She doesn't know what to feel right now, and I can't bear to watch her struggle much longer. She likes you, Daniel. I can sense she's thinking about you when she's with me. I want you to be with her, because you're a good guy."

"But—"

"But what? Don't you want her?"

"You know I want her. But what about you?"

"Oh, I'll be fine. I've already got some new subs lined up. Good girls. Girls in need of discipline. Wednesday has reached a point in her life where she needs something more, something I can't give her. Something besides...training." He raised an eyebrow at Daniel.

"Something I think you can give her. In return, all I ask is that you keep me apprised of how she is, so that in some small way I can still be part of her life. Not that you could tell her that, obviously."

"Keep you *apprised*? What do you mean? Spy on her for you? Feed you reports?"

"Reports? No, I would just want you to tell me, generally, how she's doing. If she's happy. How her life is. That she's safe." Vincent leaned closer and looked him in the eyes. "I want you to love her and baby her and discipline her and marry her and get her pregnant with little Daniels and Wednesdays—"

"Wait, stop." Daniel's head spun. "You can't...you can't just give her to me like she's some *thing*, some property of yours to pass on."

"Can't I? Daniel, I already have. I brought you to her, and as I suspected, she fell for you. And you like her. In fact, you want her desperately, don't you?"

Daniel sat in stony silence. Of course he did.

"Well then. She's yours. I give her to you."

Goddamn it.

"Look," Vincent said. "Let's not make this complicated. I'm going to break up with her, and you're going to gather up the pieces."

"Gather up the pieces, huh? Just like that? What makes you so sure she's going to fall swooning into my arms?"

"Because I know her. I know her like I know myself. I know she shouldn't be alone, and I know what she needs to be happy." He paused, glaring viciously at a spot on the floor. "She thinks she'd be happy with me forever, but she won't be. She shouldn't be..."

Daniel took a hard look at him.

"So the whole time—this whole thing...last week—you were planning this. When you invited me to your house."

"Yes. I had a feeling you were the one for her. I needed to see you together to be certain. And yes, you are."

"Why? Why me? How did you know?"

"Because I watched you at the clubs. I talked to girls you'd been with, and I talked to you. I've known you a long time. I used to be your teacher."

"Yes, I remember. You were a good teacher," he said grudgingly.

"Look, Daniel. I chose you mainly because I trust you. More than anything else, I don't want her to get hurt. You'll understand what I mean when you're with her. She won't be safe until she's with someone like you."

"Someone like me? What does that mean?"

"Someone who loves to give pleasure and affection as much as pain. She's a hard masochist, you see. Physically *and* emotionally. She'll want you to push her up to a line, then she'll want you to shove her over it." He fixed Daniel with a warning look. "You shouldn't shove her too far. She's had enough hardship in her life. Daddy issues, broken family, the self-esteem mess." He waved a hand. "You know, like so many of them. Only in her case, probably worse."

"What are you talking about? How much worse?"

He sighed. "Don't bring it up with her. It only makes her morbid. She lost her mother when she was young, and her father was a real—how shall I say this?—asshole. Suffice it to say, she's a vulnerable spirit. She needs a trustworthy person, you understand? I think she needs you. And I know you want her." Vincent leaned back and cleared his throat, looking around as if their conversation was over, as if everything that needed to be said had been said.

Daniel scratched the back of his neck, still not quite believing this conversation. "Sometimes you're really fucked-up, Vincent."

"I'm no such thing. Anyway, I'll break up with her shortly. In a month or two. I don't want to be rash. After five years, there's a process."

Daniel rolled his eyes. "If she's smart, she'll break up with you first."

"She won't break up with me. That's the whole point. God, it can be such a burden for the Dominant, caring for these hapless submissives."

"Hmm." Daniel was hard-pressed not to laugh out loud at Vincent's posturing. In fact, if he hadn't understood exactly how much Vincent loved Wednesday, he would have walked out of the office five minutes ago. As it was, Daniel was inclined to take him up on his profane game of pass-the-submissive.

And really, his motives weren't exactly selfless. He hoped Vincent broke up with her quickly. He couldn't wait to touch her again. He couldn't wait to own her. He hoped she wanted him too.

In his exhilarated mood, he tried not to think too hard about the weight of Vincent's loss and the way he tried to hide it. He tried not to think about the old man's forced smile, fixed and grim.

* * *

It was six thirty on Friday night, and Wednesday was preparing to see her Master. She'd plucked, waxed, soaked, showered, and perfumed her body to his standing specifications. Then she put on the sheer, sleek lingerie. The black bustier, the matching silk panties. She put on her makeup last, when her tears had mostly been shed, but still, one or two managed to escape.

Tonight she and Vincent were meeting to say good-bye. Like everything between them, this good-bye had been planned and agreed upon with thoughtful negotiation. It didn't make it any easier to bear.

Oh God. She was already falling apart, and he hadn't even arrived yet. *Pull it together, Wed. Don't be pathetic.* She busied herself with dusting nonexistent dust, straightening things that were already straight, and picking invisible lint off the floor. Her studio apartment was generally clean all the time, but with Vincent coming over, it seemed appropriate to make it absolutely pristine. She'd spent so many years trying to be flawless for him, and her apartment could be nothing less. She moved a picture frame one millionth of a degree to the right. *Is it straight? Is it perfect?*

Then he knocked at the door and—silly girl that she was—that knock of Vincent's brought tears to her eyes. So perfectly modulated, not too loud or too soft. Two sharp knocks, not too long or short or staccato. Those two knocks were Vincent, and she knew, like everything else that night, that she would never forget them.

She opened the door with her head bowed, partly to hide her tears, but mostly out of long-developed respect. He was her Master after all, and she his girl, and nights like these called for the consummate playing of roles. He stroked her cheek softly, just for a second, then tilted her face up to his. She gazed into dark, familiar eyes.

"Wednesday."

She swallowed hard, steeling herself against weeping. He had already brushed past. She closed and locked the door before turning and dropping to her knees.

Vincent looked around her apartment, his face betraying nothing. She waited on her knees, watching to be told what to do. He had brought nothing with him, and she felt a strange disappointment in that. She'd secretly hoped he'd tote everything over here, all the instruments of torture he'd ever used on her. She'd imagined him using them all on her one last time, one big conflagration of pain to mark the end of them, like the huge, jaw-dropping display that ended every fireworks show. But no, he most definitely had brought nothing, unless he had some nipple clamps stowed in his pocket.

She knelt, wishing she could go to him, wishing he would put his hands on her. But he did nothing, and she started to fear he might only say good-bye and walk out the door. She bit her tongue to keep from pleading with him. *Please take me. Please hold me close before you go.*

But he wasn't leaving and he wasn't moving. She tried to read him, to read if he felt anger or sadness or perhaps relief. But as usual, she could read nothing. She never could unless he wanted her to.

But her—he could read her like a book. Surely he knew exactly how hard she was fighting tears, how desperate she was to pour out her heart. He knew she wanted him to come to her. She was sure he even knew she was trying to read him, and how frustrated she was at her usual lack of success.

As it was, here and now, awaiting his words of farewell, she was barely keeping it together. Her breath was catchy, and her knees, if she hadn't been on them, would probably have collapsed.

"Stand up, Wednesday," Vincent said. "Let me look at you."

One last time, her mind added. *Let me look at you one last time.*

She rose with her arms at her sides the way he'd taught her, standing still and straight, her back slightly arched. He came over and stood behind her, yanking her panties down and letting them fall to the floor. He ran his hand over her ass, cupping each cheek. A subtle pressure on her hips, and she was down on her knees again, bending forward while he knelt behind her, unfastening his pants. She heard the faint rattle of a condom wrapper. She waited, open and ready to take him, and a moment later he slipped inside. He fucked her pussy slow and deep, his back curved over hers. Any pleasure she might have felt was stifled by a smothering grief. His fingers slipped over her skin, there but not quite there, like him. He was so uncharacteristically tender that she started to cry again.

"Don't." He pulled her back against him, his lips beside her ear. "Enough. This is because of you."

She shook her head, but if he said it, then it was true, and he was no longer gentle after that. He pulled out of her pussy and positioned the head of his cock at her ass. She tried to relax and let it happen, although there was always that moment of nervous dread. Despite the lube still on the condom, it hurt like a slow burn when he fell forward and slid in.

She felt punished by the way he used her, just as she wanted to feel. Vincent always knew what she needed when she needed it. He always knew just how to make her *feel*. When she'd first met him, her feelings had been fuzzy and unformed, as if cushioned in bubble wrap. Now they were sharp and deep, like the jab of a knife.

When Vincent finished with her ass, he pulled away silently with a light touch of fingertips. She stayed on her knees, her forehead to the floor. She was not aroused, although she always settled into a kind of serene satisfaction when he used her for his pleasure. She felt privileged to be used by him, to satisfy his urges. She hadn't even thought about coming, hadn't even begun the climb.

Now she listened and waited with trained alertness as Vincent sat on the bed. When he gave the word, she turned to take off his condom and toss it in the trash. Never in five years had he used her without one, although he'd done tests, blood work to prove he was clean. He was her only partner, but she was not his, so, in deference to that inequality, he protected her.

He protected her in many ways actually, many of which she would probably never even know. Pain and pleasure, jeopardy and protection, *I love you...but not like that.* Complicated—but she understood, as did he. Would anyone else ever understand her? She couldn't bear to think about that.

She resumed her previous position, her hands curled into fists beside her head. She felt the lack of cuffs, the lack of a collar, with devastating clarity. She hoped he might bring them and leave them with her, a souvenir of their time together. She had nothing, absolutely nothing of him, save her memories and a few, very few, ghostly pale stripes of scars across her ass. Even that she was sure he wished she didn't have. When he was gone, he would be truly and utterly *gone.* There was no hope in her mind that they would reconcile. This was the most final good-bye she'd ever participated in. Even the good-bye to her father as she'd stared down into his casket had not felt so acute.

After a few moments—she had no idea how many—Vincent came and sat beside her and ran his fingers up and over her back. Lightly, so lightly. He'd taken off his clothes and come to her naked. She could feel the warmth emanating from his skin. She wanted to touch him, every inch of him. She wanted to throw her arms around him and plead with him—

"Wednesday," he said. It was at that moment, when he breathed her name in something akin to reverence, that she realized he might have been in danger of falling apart too. But such an occurrence would have traumatized her, and fortunately he held himself together and took another quiet breath.

He unfastened her bustier and set it aside, then touched her for a long time as she knelt there. She was perfectly still, just taking in the soothing, familiar sensation of his caresses. He traced his fingertips over her ass, the curve of her hips, the round hollows of her shoulders, then he reached beneath her to fondle and squeeze her breasts. Eventually he worked his fingers into the back of her hair, and he pulled, hard enough to tell her what he wanted. She sat up and moved to him, and he guided her over his lap. He spanked her for a while, but he was never much of a straight spanker. He stopped after a few moments, when she had barely warmed up.

"Go and bring me your hairbrush." She stood and went to fetch it, then handed it over with a sigh. She hated hairbrushes.

He held her hard as he paddled her with the rigid, stinging back of the brush. The numbness of grief was replaced by the searing, stinging torture of her ass cheeks. The cracks sounded loud in the silence of her apartment, coming one on top of the other, and her ass started to burn like hell. She jumped and fidgeted, trying to evade the raining blows. Even after all this time, she couldn't help it. Pain was still her enemy, because her mind wanted it as much as her body fought against it. He held her fast, taking all choice away from her. It was one of the reasons she needed him so much.

It was a hard spanking, one of the hardest ever, as she'd expected it to be. *Something to remember me by*, he told her wordlessly, each time he brought the hairbrush down on her ass. About halfway through she began to cry. It was no slow trickle of tears; it was a waterfall. A dam breaking, a storm spitting down rain. It was anguish and catharsis unwinding inside her, letting her breathe again.

She drew in deep, shuddering gasps until he put down the brush. She relaxed over his hard thighs, the pain of good-bye forgotten, replaced with the torment of a hard, inescapable spanking. He stroked her hair, letting her calm herself. She shuddered as he traced the rising welts. He pulled her onto the bed then, and she lay on her stomach, but he stopped her and turned her over onto her back.

Her eyes and cheeks were still wet with tears, and she winced as her tender ass came to rest against the sheet. He parted her legs and began to stroke the sensitive skin between her thighs, then her clit, eliciting hot little stings of craving. He slid his fingers over it with masterful dexterity. Her pussy was wet and burning hot, but she shivered as he looked down at her.

Then he dipped his lips to her body, sucking on her clit and blazing a slow, deliberate trail across her slick folds with his tongue. The pleasure unhinged her, made it hard to think. She wanted to come, she wanted to wail, but she was unsure of what he wanted her to do. He had taken her this way, with his mouth, few enough times that she was at a loss.

"Put your hands over your head, Wednesday. Leave them there."

She did as he said, and he wrapped his hands around her ass cheeks, pulling her closer. Then he lowered his mouth to her again. Hard and soft bites, and licks to soothe the ache away. Flowering sensation and building bliss. Her hips jerked of their own accord, inching forward as far as he would let them to greedily take the pleasure he gave. She made noises that embarrassed her. He was relentless, teasing her and bringing her to the edge again and again.

Then he parted her legs even farther, almost past comfort. "Stay."

She stayed, a quivering pile of conquered, dazed girl. He looked down at her from beside the bed while he rolled on a condom, then he climbed between her legs. He gathered her in his arms, tender again. She was limp with pleasure, and he slid inside her with ease. She knew the feel of him inside her like a brand. She knew the hot, slick solidity of him by heart. She clenched at him with her pussy since she couldn't touch him with her fingers.

His rough, crisp chest hair slid across her breasts, and his breath whispered against her neck like a secret. He seemed to drive deeper, hotter. He stretched and used her, and her body responded, burning for him. He held her close and fucked her, body to body, chest to chest, stomach to stomach, and she thought she would just die. *You have to remember,* she thought. *You have to remember this feeling of him inside.* He had been the very first man inside her, and he had taken her just like this, close and slow, wrapped in his arms. It still felt like that first time, urgent yet restrained.

They moved together there on her bed, his authority and her submission seeming to fall away, leaving only raw connection. Her breaths were his breaths, and his hands were her hands. His lips found hers, and he kissed her with passionate insistence. He tasted of her. She was falling apart, shaking, climbing to a terrifying apex. "Come, Wednesday," he whispered against her lips. "I love how you look when you come."

She let go, gritting her teeth against the overpowering climax. She let it wash over her, clenching her fists and crying out as if it hurt. In some sense it did hurt. It hurt to realize she would never again feel this close to him. For a long time afterward, he lay still on top of her, breathing in and breathing out. She counted time by the beats of his heart. *Remember, remember. Remember his weight on you, the scent of him, the tickle of his chest hair, the brush of his breath against your ear.*

He finally rose and stood over her. "Kneel beside the bed," he said, authoritative as always. She knelt, wrung-out and overwhelmed with emotion. He didn't beckon her to remove and discard his condom, but did it himself. Then he began to dress with a mechanical detachment. She watched as he buttoned his shirt, put on his pants and cashmere sweater. He adjusted his collar and reached down to buckle his belt. Just like that, his body was gone from her. He sat on the bed again and leaned down to pull on his socks and shoes. As he straightened, he made a gesture for her to approach him.

"Kneel here, before me. Face me with your hands in your lap."

She crawled the short distance to the point he indicated, her legs shaky from too much pleasure. She looked up at him, her eyes dewy and her heart aching in her chest.

"Don't cry," he said. "Don't talk. Just listen."

He leaned forward and cupped her cheek, then kissed her on both her eyelids, more gently than he ever had. She took a deep breath, drifting on the scent of him and the tender, fleeting sensations.

"Thank you, Wednesday, for everything. I'll miss you."

I'll miss you too, she wanted to cry out. *I'll miss you so much! I don't know how I'll survive without you.*

"I wish you the greatest happiness in life," he continued. "I wish you love and inspiration. A soul mate, to know and understand you. You'll get it. Don't settle."

She bit the inside of her cheek to stay silent. She could feel his lips, soft and yet hard, brushing against her lids. She looked at the ceiling, at the walls, then at him. *Please let me speak. Let me say it all.* She started to open her mouth, to tell him everything, or even just one thing: *thank you.*

"No," he said. "No." One word, *no*, but in their economical language she understood the myriad layers of it.

No, I want to remember you as you are.

No, we're saying good-bye. Let's not risk this.

No, you'll say something you'll regret.

No, there are not enough words for the weight of this moment anyway.

So she knelt, hot with sadness and unshed tears, and ground her teeth to keep from weeping. Even so, a few tears escaped and rolled down her cheeks. They were ignored. Soon after, with one last kiss to her forehead, he stood and left, closing the door behind him.

All the words that longed to spring from her tongue were forever silenced. No matter. In the way he had of understanding everything about her, she was sure he knew exactly what she felt, exactly what she would have said down to the last syllable.

He knew exactly what she would have said if she could have, which is why, probably, he insisted on her silence until the bitter end.

3 CHAPTER THREE

"Thanks," Daniel said to the waitress as she set down the coffee.

"Sure, Mr. Laurent."

He rattled his paper and furtively checked his watch.

Seven fifty-five.

Almost time.

He didn't do this every day. He wasn't that pathetic. But yes, he did it often enough that the wait staff knew him by name. He did it often enough that he knew she got in to work around eight, and left to walk home every evening at five. He didn't watch her leave very often, though. The temptation was just too great, the temptation to cross the street and "run into" her. It would have been so easy, so quick.

But no. He'd been giving her some space. He didn't want to try to woo her while she was still processing the hurt of Vincent's uncollaring, so instead he planned and waited. The first move had to be controlled. No precipitous propositions. No wild declarations of desire.

God, there she was, right there, all legs and short skirt and wild hair and her too-big messenger bag banging against her hip. He could have eaten her alive. Every day he wanted to go to her, cross the street and lay claim to her, but he only watched her disappear into her office, biding his time.

Until today.

It had been over a month since Vincent let her go. Every day that went by was one day closer she got to mental health. She barely dragged anymore. In fact, yesterday he'd sensed an alarming new energy to her gait. God forbid she'd meet some other nice guy before he'd put in his bid.

So why did he still sit here spying? Fuck, why was this so difficult? Why not just walk up to her, shake her hand? *Remember me? You sucked me off once. It was great. Then I fucked you, two times actually. And I spanked you over my lap just to make your Master mad.* So maybe it would require more finesse than that. He was the king of finesse. He worked in the film business, for God's sake. He had to schmooze and manipulate directors and producers on a regular basis, and he was very good at what he did. Producers loved his work.

But what about Wednesday? Had she loved his work? She seemed to that night, but with submissives it was hard to tell. Most of them pretended they liked stuff even when they didn't—a necessary evil, he supposed, when you lived to serve. He knew for sure, though, that he'd made her orgasm. She'd come for him, with him, more than once that night. He'd felt it, felt the delicious squeeze and shudder. Something that strong, even Wednesday couldn't fake.

Enough waiting. He screwed up his Dominant mojo and crossed the street. He was stepping onto the sidewalk outside her office when the door flew open. She jumped back in shock while he stood and stared at her. He hadn't seen her close up like this, not for months. She rendered him speechless with those otherworldly eyes, and there he stood, not a word, not a movement. She looked back at him as if she'd seen a ghost.

"Hi," he finally managed to spit out. *Brilliant. More please, before she runs.* "Wednesday, right? Do you remember me?"

"Yes. Of course I do."

"You work here? I remember you said you were an editor." *You remember, that night you and I fucked? God, smile at me, please.*

"Yes, I've worked here for a couple of years now."

I know. I've actually been stalking you for about, oh, two months of that time. "I was just passing by. God, it's good to see you."

"It's good to see you too."

She said that as if she'd rather see anyone, *anyone else* on earth. Had he imagined it, their connection? He tried to read her. She looked totally scared.

"Listen, I guess this feels weird, since the last time...the last time we were together..."

"Yeah," she said. "It does feel a little weird."

"I just want you to know—" What did he want her to know? God, so many things. "I want you to know that I really had fun that night. I mean, I thought you did too."

She made a faint noise of agreement or assent, and looked around.

He pressed on, wanting to explain. "I mean, it was more than just fun to me. Maybe this isn't the place to discuss this, out here on the street."

"Probably. I'd better be getting home."

"Can I walk with you?"

She frowned, but didn't say anything when he fell into step beside her.

"I heard you and Vincent broke up."

"Yes. About a month ago."

"I'm sorry to hear that. You made a good couple. He loved you very much, I could tell."

"We were never a couple, and Vincent never loved me."

"Didn't he?" Daniel wondered if she believed that. "Well, I don't know much about you and Vincent, but I was grateful to him for sharing you with me."

"Do you do that a lot?" she asked. "The sharing thing?"

"I'd never done it before you. It's not usually my thing."

"But you and Vincent shared me."

"Yes. Unfortunately for you."

"Unfortunately? Why do you say that?"

"I think I got you in a fair bit of hot water that night. And drew a few tears from you, if memory serves me right."

Blush, blush, blush, and that soft laugh.

"Yes. You made me cry a little bit, over your lap. Just a little."

"I've been told that I spank too hard."

"By whom? Not your submissive?"

It was his turn to laugh at her scandalized expression. Vincent, that old dog, had trained this one well. "More than a few girls have yelled it at me before they stormed out of my house."

"I would never storm out on someone," she said.

"How do you know? You've only been with one man, haven't you?"

"I was with more than one man."

"Sure, men Vincent carefully selected for you. You don't think he invited just anyone from the clubs?"

She shrugged. "I don't know. I don't care. Honestly, I'm trying to move on."

"Are you seeing someone new?"

"No. I don't want to, not yet. I'm not even sure I'm into that BDSM crap anymore."

"Really?" That surprised him. Her entire lack of enthusiasm for his existence surprised him. He studied her, trying to find the right words to say. "It would be a shame for you to leave the lifestyle. You're good at it."

She made a bitter sound, something between a snort and a laugh. "I'm not so sure about that. I wasn't good enough for Vincent."

Daniel narrowed his eyes. He wanted to destroy Vincent for causing the bleak look on Wednesday's face. "Did he tell you that?"

"No. He said something about me moving on, finding a soul mate or happiness or something. It was the classic 'it's not you, it's me' thing. But whatever. The bottom line is I'm not in a real hurry to get into another D/s relationship."

"I can understand that, with all you've been through. I'm disappointed to hear it, though. I had hoped you and I might give things a try."

She walked a little faster. "I don't know."

"Wednesday, I'm nothing at all like Vincent. I actually think you and I would be a much better fit."

"You seemed a lot like Vincent that night."

"I mean, yes, I am like Vincent in some ways. I'm a D-type and a sadist. I like kinky sex and exchanging power. But I want more than that, too."

They walked in silence for a moment. This wasn't how he'd imagined their long-awaited reunion. She was so pent-up, so defensive. He put a hand on her arm, a soft touch that nonetheless stopped her. She looked down at the sidewalk between them.

"What do you want, Wednesday? Where do you want to go next in life?"

"I don't know. That's what I'm trying to explain to you. I don't know what I want right now."

God, that was obvious. He wanted to take her in his arms, strip her naked, lay her down, and make all her fears go away. Instead he said, "Let me help you figure things out."

"How? Scenes in your playroom?" He could guess what she thought of that idea from the pinched set of her mouth.

"I don't have a playroom. Or collars, or a dungeon with bolts in the walls. I'm not like him. I want something different."

"Something different? What does that mean?"

"I don't know how to sum it up in a few words, but I'd like to talk to you more about it. If you'd like." He took her hand loosely, and she let him, leaving it cool and still in his. "We had a connection that night. You felt it as much as I did."

"Daniel—"

"Didn't you? Answer me."

"Yes," she said. "I guess I did feel something, but that was another time, months ago."

"I still feel the same. And I think you do too. I think you're scared."

"Yes, I am scared! I'm not even fully over Vincent yet, and this is...so soon—too soon."

"We can take things slowly. We can take our time."

"Can we?" she asked, cocking one eyebrow at him.

Touché. "We can try."

"I don't know." She tossed her head, a nervous, panicked gesture. "I have to go. I'm sorry."

God, he didn't want to let her go, not like this. "Wait. Let me take you to dinner tomorrow night. Just one dinner, and if you say it can't happen, if there's nothing there, I'll leave you alone. But can't we at least talk, you and me? Not here on the street, but over dinner. Yes? Please?" He pressed her, full benevolent-Dominant mode. It was now or never.

"Okay," she said. "I guess we can have dinner."

She said okay, but she sounded far from enthused.

* * *

Oh God, let me breathe now. Please give me breath. Daniel—Daniel—was arriving soon to take her out to dinner. Daniel, whom she had dreamed about so many countless hours before she realized he wasn't coming back to find her. Daniel, who wanted to be with her after all. She didn't know whether to celebrate or cry.

She'd only just resigned herself to letting it all go, the BDSM, the idea of finding another Dominant. She'd begun looking forward to a lifetime alone eating tons of ice cream and collecting stray cats. She was finally okay with it, then there he was outside her office like some kind of specter. He'd been sexier and more compelling than ever, impossible to resist.

She should have pretended she hadn't seen him, and kept walking. Would he have let her go? No. He'd seemed quite insistent on talking to her. In fact, she wondered if he had just happened to be there, or if it had been planned.

Either way, she'd let herself talk to him, which was mistake number one. She'd let him walk home with her, spilling words in her ear, words that had convinced her, almost, that it was a good idea to try again at the lifestyle. The lifestyle of belonging to someone, giving herself over to someone day in and day out, that lifestyle of lying in bed or kneeling or standing bolted to the wall, waiting to be done to. That lifestyle she was finished with—he made her want it back. "We can take things slow," he'd assured her, but they were already past slow. They had been past slow the very moment they'd met.

She stood against the door, breathing in and out, trying to calm herself. She dreaded belonging so soon already to another man. The belonging was exciting to her, yes, but still dangerous. Even Vincent, who'd held her at arm's length, had managed to take over her life. He had taken over her, made her not completely her own, and Daniel seemed to hint at wanting something even deeper, an actual relationship. Commitment. Love. The idea fascinated yet repulsed her. It alarmed her. She was so used to keeping her emotions stuffed down.

She was all in black, from head to toe and underneath. She was in mourning for the death of her attempt to find herself, to take some time for herself. Time was up. She had swept her hair up in a loose chignon so he could look all he wanted at her neck. She imagined for a moment his thick fingers smoothing a black collar against her skin.

She could almost feel his rough fingertips grazing her nape, working the clasp...

Oh Jesus. She hadn't wanted this. But she did. She *did*. Didn't she? She had to get ahold of herself before he came to the door. Then, right on cue, there was the knock against her back. Daniel was there, now, on the other side of the door. Where had she heard that knock before, not too loud or too soft? Not too long or too short or staccato? *Don't think of him now.* She took one last deep breath of freedom and picked up her small black bag.

She opened the door almost warily and let him into her apartment. Daniel. He looked just as amazing as always. Dark jacket, crisp white shirt, a tie the exact color of his beautiful eyes. Classic, masculine style. He seemed like such a virile man standing there that she had to fight the urge to drop to her knees. He moved closer, took her hand, and nuzzled against her cheek.

She floundered, she floated. She almost fainted. Vincent had never greeted her quite this way. Daniel's cheek was warm against hers, slightly rough, and his lips... She was acutely aware of the place they pressed just below her ear. She felt his chest brush against hers for a second.

He stepped away and made a gallant gesture in the direction of the door. "Shall we go?"

"Yes," she said. *Or we won't go anywhere at all.*

* * *

Wednesday sat beside him in the car, tense and still, and he could feel the protective shield drawn around her. He reached over and took her hand in his.

"What's the matter?"

"Nothing. I'm just... You'll laugh at me," she said with a shake of her head.

"I won't laugh at you. Tell me what's wrong."

"I've never actually been on a sort of...you know..."

"Date?"

"Yes, if that's——"

"Yes, that is what this is, Wednesday. A date. A man takes a woman out to dinner and talks to her and pulls out her chair and pays for the check."

"I mean, Vincent took me out sometimes, but it was mostly..."

"Foreplay for his threesomes?"

"You're laughing at me."

"No, I'm not laughing. I don't find this funny in the slightest, I promise you. Vincent——" He clamped his mouth shut. He was about to say *Vincent wronged you* or perhaps even *Vincent mistreated you*, but tearing down her longtime lover and his eccentricities probably wasn't the way to ingratiate himself.

When they were seated at their dark and private table, she perched on the edge of her chair and looked around in a daze, as if she'd suddenly, inexplicably fallen into real life. Like Alice down the rabbit hole. *Now what do I do, what do I do?* He wanted to reassure her. *This is how men treat women in the real world. This is how men treat women whom they want to know. And I do want to know you, Wednesday. I want to know you very well.*

She was even more beautiful than he remembered. She wore a sweet black dress that made his breath catch, and her pretty lips were curved in an anxious little smile. He was probably nearly as nervous as she was, but he tried to hide it. He had to be the one in control.

He was the one who had to convince her that she needed and wanted to come where he led.

The menus arrived, and he ordered wine and dinner for both of them, and that—*you'll eat what I tell you to eat*—at least seemed to put her at ease. Dominance 101: Order for your submissive. Take away her choices in the insignificant things, but learn what really matters to her and work your ass off to give her that.

"So, Wednesday," he said, leaning back in his chair. "Tell me about yourself."

"What would you like to know?"

"Everything. I'd like to know everything."

She laughed. "There's an awful lot to know."

Good girl. So she had retained at least some shred of self-identity. "What do you like to do when you're not on your knees?"

She blushed. "I like to write. And I like movies. Good ones, not stupid ones."

"I like movies too. We have that in common."

"Tell me about your work. I've seen some of the film sets you designed. I love your style—"

He cut her off gently. "Thank you, but we're talking about you. What else do you like to do besides write? You like to read, I assume?"

"I read a lot, yeah. I work a lot too."

"You like your job?"

"Yes. It's really rewarding, editing people's writing. It's a big responsibility. They give it over to you when it's so personal and meaningful to them. Entrust you with it, to improve it. I don't know. It's hard to explain."

"I understand. Taking care of something given over to you in trust." She met his eyes. *Trust me.* "I'm sure you're very good at it, Wednesday."

"I try to be."

"So do I."

She fell silent again, his tense black flower.

"What else?" he asked. "Surely you do more than work and write."

She shrugged. "I like to work out."

"You like to work out? Most people find it a chore."

"I like to sit and...think. I like to just think about things sometimes for hours. I'm boring, I know."

"No, you certainly aren't. What do you think about when you think about things for hours?"

She balked then. He could practically hear the inner monologue. *You can't have my thoughts. You can have everything else, but not that.*

"Okay," he said. "Tell me this. What did you think about last night as you fell asleep?" He lowered his voice. "Did you think about me?"

Her gaze skittered away from his. "Yes."

"Tell me what you thought about."

"I thought about tonight. What we would talk about. How it would be to...be here with you. How it would be...if..."

"If you were mine? I was thinking about that too. I've been thinking about it for quite some time, actually. Since the night I met you. It's been a long, long time to think."

"I know. It has." She stared down at the table and took a small sip of wine.

"Let me tell you what I've been thinking about, Wednesday. Look at me, please. When I talk to you, I'd like you to look at me." Just like that, the authority crystallized in his voice, and he'd already taught her a rule. She took a deep breath and obeyed, and his gaze held hers.

"Before we take this any further, I'm going to be blunt with you. An arrangement like you and Vincent shared would not be enough to satisfy me."

"I know. That's why I feel kind of scared."

That quiet, open admission gave him hope for them. "Thank you for being honest. I'll always want you to tell me how you feel. One of my kinks, I suppose," he said with a half-smile. "I'm going to want to know you inside and out."

"If I'm going to be yours."

"If you're going to be mine. You see, the better I know you, the more easily I can..." He almost said *love you*, but thought better of it and said, "The more easily I can make you happy." For him, loving and being happy were the same thing. For her, well...he wasn't so sure. "Have you ever been in love?"

"No, I never have."

"Why?" *Open up to me, Wednesday. Tell me.*

"I guess because love is so messy. It makes people strange."

He couldn't hide his smile at that, although he tried to. "So what you and Vincent had—that wasn't strange?"

"You disapprove of Vincent." She frowned. "You disapprove of me for staying with him so long."

"I'd prefer if you didn't tell me what I approve or disapprove of. I only want to express to you that Vincent and I are different, as different as night and day. I'm sure he was an excellent Dominant to you, but you'll find I'm not much like him."

"Yes, that's pretty clear to me already."

Their food arrived then. They ate in tense silence as he retreated, regrouped. Things weren't going well. By this point he'd thought they'd be discussing preferences, specifics, how she would address him, what she would wear, the days they would get together. Instead he was racking his brain for a way to salvage things.

When the silence grew ridiculous, he fell back on the only thing he could think of. "You know, this is what he wanted for you. What he wanted you to find." She didn't have to ask who *he* was. He might as well have been sitting at the table with them. "Do you still love him so much? Is it really too soon for us?"

"I didn't love him. I don't."

"You did. You do. You'd return to him right now if he'd let you."

She looked up at him as if she'd been slapped, then turned away, completely closed off. She placed her utensils beside her plate.

Dinner had been an unparalleled disaster.

Daniel sighed loud and long and signaled the waiter for the check.

Chapter Four

He drove her home in tense silence. Was he giving up? Not even. For the moment he was—he would give her some time and space, then he'd try again. He escorted her to her apartment door, and was going to bid her good night, when she looked up at him with tears in her eyes.

Tears. Fucking tears from this woman. From any woman, but especially this one.

"Wednesday, don't..." he said, but it was too late then. Too late.

He pushed her inside her apartment, shut the door, and took her in his arms. He kissed her hard, trapping her hands at the small of her back, both of her hands that fit perfectly in one of his. With the other hand, he pressed her nape, drawing her closer, tasting her, taking what he'd fantasized about for so many months.

Finally she pulled away, but he didn't let go. With a sigh, she pressed her body against his and rested her head on his shoulder.

"I'm sorry, I'm sorry," she whispered. "You know, I want it, but I don't want it. I can't explain. I don't understand it myself."

"Shh, it's okay. I understand. I do. Just trust me. For now, just trust me." He nuzzled her cheek, and she turned her face up to his, offering her lips. He kissed her thoroughly, voraciously. This time, he broke away.

"Turn around," he said in an urgent voice, hoping she'd obey. And wonder of wonders, she did. He kept her hands trapped in his. Gently but firmly he pressed her shoulders against the wall, telling her without words not to move. With his other hand, slowly, oh, so slowly, he traced a line down her back, over the curve of her hips, then dropped his fingertips to the tops of her thighs. He inched up her dress's hem with steady pressure. She let him do all these things, standing still with her back trembling against his front.

He was harder than he'd ever been in his life, wild with desire, but somehow he managed to only touch her. What he really wanted to do was tear off her dress and thrust deep inside. He only inched that hem up little by little, caressing her velvet thighs as he went. She clenched her hands inside his, and she tensed as he hooked his fingers in the top of her panties.

"Be still," he whispered. "Just let me touch you."

She shivered as he eased her panties down to the tops of her stockings, and left them to rest at the apex of her thighs.

"Part your legs." She obeyed with a soft, excited sound. He traced his fingers down her front, caressing her intimately, exploring every lovely fold and crevice of her slick center. As he cupped her mons, he pressed his hips forward against her ass. His raging hard-on nestled perfectly between her ass cheeks. She took deep, halting breaths, her hands still trapped in his, between them, in fists.

He delved lower, past her swollen clit to the moisture, hot and wet, between her legs. He dipped his fingers inside her.

"Daniel," she whimpered.

He tightened the hand that trapped her wrists, and lowered his head to whisper against her cheek. "Wednesday, be my submissive. Give me as much as you can give me, and I'll live with that. For a while, anyway."

"Okay," she said. "Yes. Okay."

"I'll never hurt you. Trust me, and you and I, we'll figure things out."

Later. They would figure things out later. For now, he fumbled into one of the condoms he'd secreted in his wallet in hopes he might need it before the night was through. He fucked her there against the wall, grasping and artless. His nerves sang at the feel of her skin sliding against his.

He couldn't touch her enough. He couldn't get close enough. When she came with a gasp, when she tensed beneath him, he remembered that night at Vincent's and all the longing he'd done since then. All he could think was *I can't let her go.*

Afterward they slid to the floor, and he knelt over her and whispered it in her ear. "Mine. You're mine," as if he needed to convince her. He helped her up, pulled her dress over her head, and led her straight to the bed.

"What do you have that I can tie you up with?"

Wednesday thought a moment. "Stockings?"

"Too stretchy. I need something stronger."

She didn't have anything he could use, so he did what any desperate pervert would have done. He took a pair of scissors to her sheets. "I'll replace them," he said. She looked at him like he was crazy as he cut off the four long strips. Wrist, wrist, ankle, ankle. Enough for now. He had to tie this girl down.

"Come. Lie down here," he said, patting the middle of the bed. She crawled to the place he showed her in her sexy black lingerie and shoes, her naughty little ass right up in the air. Delicious tease. Her hair was a mess now, all disheveled and falling down in strands around her face. The sight of her kneeling on the bed drove him to madness. He had to be inside her again.

Patience. Soon. "Lie down on your back. Put your arms up."

She did without a moment's pause. Her eyes were shining with desire as he took one wrist and fixed it to the headboard, and started to wrap the cotton strip around it in a knot she'd never be able to undo. The bonds were props, metaphor only. She was his, and after he finished with her that night, she'd be his even more. "I suppose now would be the time to discuss a safe word," he said as he finished the first knot.

"I don't need a safe word," she said. "I trust you."

"Even so, we're going to have one at first. Don't be a foolish little submissive. You're too trusting."

She smiled, gazing up at him. "Are you going to hurt me?"

He frowned back. "This isn't a joke. Either you pick a safe word, or I will." He tied her other wrist tighter, then knelt at the edge of the bed to remove her shoes and tie her ankles. Her twin bed was too small to spread her as he wanted her, but it would have to do. For now.

"How about 'untie me, Daniel'? Not that you'll ever use it, you reckless girl. But there it is, if you need it."

"Okay." She squirmed, testing her bonds to see how tight they were. *See? I'm not fucking around.*

He sat beside her, still fully dressed, and stroked her cheek. "Now, what am I going to do with you?"

"You're the Dominant."

"It was a rhetorical question. Hush."

She was a vision on the bed, her black stockings in sharp contrast with her white sheets. He touched her, starting with the velvet curve between her shoulder and neck. He moved down to her breasts, cupping and massaging them. He closed his fingers on the sensitive skin of her nipples and squeezed until he got the reaction he wanted—a protest. Her lips stayed closed tight, but she pulled away to the extent she could.

He made a soft sound and released her, flattening his hands against her rib cage. He could feel her short, halting breaths under his fingertips. "Did I hurt you?"

"Yes."

"*Yes, Sir.*"

"Yes, Sir," she said, squirming again. He stilled her with a pinch.

"You like to be hurt, though. Don't you? It makes you feel good."

She watched him with alert attention, as if she was trying to figure him out. It didn't surprise him—he was doing the same to her. He moved his hands lower, over the lace of her garter belt and down to the elastic suspenders. "What else do you like?"

She didn't answer. He traced across the soft skin at the tops of her thighs. She tensed as his fingers crept inward and caressed the crease of her mons. He smiled and delved one thumb between her pussy lips, then found her clit and stroked it.

"Do you like this?"

Her mouth opened, but nothing came out. Her hips reacted, though, rising, seeking more contact.

"Hmm. I see," he said. "How about this?" He slid his hands lower and parted her labia before slipping two fingers into her warm, wet channel. He felt her clench and tense again. Her face was a mask of concentration and control.

"Don't you like that?" He moved his fingers in and out, and she opened her mouth again. She arched her head back. With her halo of hair and her arms spread wide, she looked like some angel of dark lust and feeling. Still, she was staunchly silent. He moved a hand to one breast and teased the nipple again as he continued to finger-fuck her. "No words, Wednesday? How will I know what you like and don't like?"

She licked her lips and gazed at him. "I...I like what you like. I want what you want."

"What if I want to saw your head off with a pocketknife and use it as a bookend?"

She laughed softly. "Then I've seriously misjudged you."

"What if I don't want you to come? Ever? What if I like you crying and miserable?" He squeezed her nipple hard and watched her shudder. "How much pain do you really want?"

"Enough."

"Enough. That's illuminating."

"Well, I don't know. Vincent never asked me all these things. He mostly just did what he wanted."

"I'll do that too, a lot of the time. We'll have rules and protocols. You like rules and protocols?"

"I like what you like," she said.

"Okay, I get it. So I'll tell you what I like. I like obedience. I like submission. True submission, not the fuzzy-handcuff kind. I like transparency and honesty." He moved his hand down to the curve of her hip and traced it. He still caressed her center, wet and silky. She was an ocean against his hand.

"Transparency is hard for me," she whispered.

"I know. But you're the one who likes pain."

Oh, her smile was adorable. He reached up and placed his palm over the base of her neck. Her pulse beat, hard and strong. "I don't like collars much. I know you've worn one for a long time."

"You won't collar me?" The disappointment in her tone was edifying. As mixed as her signals were, on some level she wished to belong to him.

"I don't want your submission to be something you can take off and put in a drawer." He slid his palm down to rest over her heart. "If things work out between us, the bondage will be here. You understand?"

"Yes, Sir. I think I understand. But you're right," she said slowly, studying him. "You and Vincent couldn't be more different."

"We're alike in some ways." He went back to teasing her clit. She arched again, a wanton, aroused creature in black stockings, tied to the bed. His cock throbbed. He wanted to hurt her. He wanted to fuck her. "Vincent didn't let you come without permission, did he?"

She shook her head, a strained look on her face.

"I won't either. You can come when I tell you to come, and when you don't have permission, I don't want you so much as touching yourself." He smiled, working her pussy with questing, slickened fingers.

"Daniel," she whispered. "May I please come now?"

"No."

"Please." She squirmed under his touch.

He leaned over to lick one taut nipple. "I don't want you to come yet."

She sighed, somewhat irritably.

"Careful, Wednesday. Don't get petulant with me. Let's see how much control you have. Be a good girl."

"Do you really want me to be good? Or do you want me to be bad so you can punish me?"

He pinched her nipple hard. "You can be a good girl for me. Mostly good and a little bad. I won't have to treat you like shit to get off on it all. Your happiness will be enough for me."

"My happiness?" His fingers circled her clit, and she sighed.

"You want someone to please, someone to be a good girl for. Be a good girl for me, and I'll make you glad. And Wednesday...don't come."

She shook her head as if that settled things, as if by her will alone, she could obey. But his wicked will was involved too, and he couldn't wait to give her some pain. He lowered his lips to suck first one nipple, then the other. He thrust his fingers up inside her hard, in and out, rubbing over her G-spot. She made breathless, muted noises of denial and panic. He felt her hips move, felt her shiver—and felt her walls contract around his fingers. He had to give her credit. She'd made no obvious sound or indication, but he'd felt it, and her guilty eyes met his.

"I remember," he whispered conspiratorially. "Your secret orgasms. I remember them well. You'll never fool me, though, so don't even try it."

"Daniel, I want to be a good girl for you."

"You will be. Don't worry, I'll help you learn."

He untied her and retied her on her tummy. God, her ass was criminally tempting, framed as it was by the straps on the lingerie she wore. He pulled his belt out of his pants and doubled it over, then looked down at the beautiful girl on the bed, so willing to take his pain.

"I'd like you to count, Wednesday. To twenty."

* * *

Ouch! Jesus!

She thought he spanked hard. His fucking belt was even harder to deal with. *Ten. Eleven. Twelve!* Vicious, aching sting. She hadn't taken a spanking in over a month, so yes, she counted for him, but it wasn't easy. She cried and yelped between numbers, but the blows kept raining down in noisy, stinging slaps of fire. By the end she was truly struggling to hold it together, even thinking the words *Untie me, Daniel.*

But no, she didn't say them. It wasn't really a safe-word moment. It was just a spanking that had come when she was far too relaxed and loose.

To be truthful, she wanted it. She wanted him to call her his *good girl*, to punish her and correct her, then hold her and make everything okay. She wanted to feel like she couldn't take another second of pain, then have to deal with more anyway. *Thirteen, fourteen...* So much pain! Pain he wanted to give her, and pain she wanted to take. After fifteen, he put one hand on the small of her back, and the rest came in a ruthless volley that had her straining at her bonds. Her numbers tumbled over themselves. *Eighteen, nineteen!* At twenty, as promised, he stopped. He left his hand on her, caressing her ass lightly with the belt he'd used to punish her.

"Okay. Too hard or too soft?"

He was asking her? When she hesitated, he gave her another small crack on the back of her thigh, above her stocking. "Answer me. Too hard or too soft?"

"Just...just right. It was..." She was having trouble talking as the belt continued to circle her ass cheeks. She wiped the tears from her face against the smooth sheets beneath her. "It was perfect." The words probably would have sounded more convincing if they hadn't come out in a sniffling sob.

"Be honest. Don't tell me what I want to hear. I don't know much about your limits yet."

"You could...well...probably go a little bit harder."

"Look at me."

His voice was sharp. She craned her head up to meet his assessing gaze. Did he see it, everything she felt? The happiness, the sadness? The excitement and dread of her own vulnerability? He was still holding the belt. It dangled from his hand, a material symbol of his power over her. She wanted to lick it. He tightened his grip on the leather and buckle.

"Thank you, Sir, for punishing me," she whispered. "I'll try not to come without permission again, if that's what you want."

"Yes, it's what I want. All your orgasms, for me alone. No masturbation. Not even any touching. Do you understand? Mine."

She drew in a deep, shuddery breath, and nodded quickly. She couldn't have said another word without breaking into abject begging for his body, his cock. For that hand, holding that belt so carelessly. She was a solid, trembling vessel of need. Just an iota, just a hair, she pressed her hips forward. Vincent would have punished her for it, for willfulness and putting her needs before his instructions. Did it count as masturbation? Yes. She sobbed into the bed, making fists.

"Please, Sir..."

The belt dropped. She heard his clothes fall to the floor and felt the bed dip as he crawled onto the mattress behind her. She was still tied, hand and foot. She would have launched herself at him if she could have. She ground against the bed in earnest. All she cared about was that he fuck her again, right there, right then, right now. He chuckled and grasped her hips, holding her still.

"I can already see you're going to be a hard one to control."

Hard to control? He already controlled her; that must have been plain enough for him to see as she tossed around under him like a wanton slut. He already had her completely under his thumb, under his heel, wrapped around his little finger. All those trite expressions— she was all of them and more. She waited, her pussy throbbing, her ass tingling with afterburn as he rolled on a condom and then slapped her flanks a couple more times.

"I like you all sore-assed and horny," he said against her ear as he positioned himself. "I like you just like this, eager to please me."

Please, please, please.

"Do you want my cock, Wednesday?"

"Yes, Sir! Oh yes, please." Her hands strained at the cotton strips that held her tethered to the bed, and her legs pulled at the bonds around her ankles as she tried to arch back to him.

"Shhh, okay. You'll get what you want. Here, baby…" His thick cock parted her, driving inside her while she panted. His warmth and solid length replaced the craving she felt. He filled and split her. He braced his arms on either side of her head. She stared from beneath the prison of his body, fascinated by the light freckles and the dusting of fluffy blond hair on his forearm, and the veins that ran up to his elbow.

A whole new world, a whole new lover to discover. She wanted to touch him everywhere, but she couldn't. She squirmed under him, contacting him wherever she could. Her pussy gripped his cock as his hips surged forward again and again in an undulating, snapping rhythm. Each stroke was hot, sliding friction. Her pelvis was swelling, aching for release. She lost track of her room, her name, her very history. There was only her body and his, and the powerful, humbling experience of being taken by him.

"Daniel!"

"Come on, baby. Yes." He grabbed a handful of her hair and fucked her harder, faster. She was taken and overtaken. The pressure in her middle burst wide, and she clenched her teeth against the intensity of the orgasm he gave her. Waves of heat brought feral animal release as his cock thrust inside her, centering her as she clamped down on his power. Her last thought as the orgasm spun her world upside down was that it was fortunate she was tied to the bed.

When she came back from the place she'd gone, Daniel was lying beside her, alternately licking her neck and her shoulder. She stretched against him, still securely tethered.

"I suppose I have to untie you now," he whispered.

"At some point." She looked over into warm blue eyes. "Although I enjoyed being tied up by you."

"I had a feeling you did." He started working the first knot loose. She flexed her wrist with a smile, studying this man who had just dominated and possessed her so effortlessly. He was little more than a stranger, yet she felt almost painfully connected to him. His teasing gazes were already familiar. She already knew the feel of his chest hair against her skin and the bronze color of the freckles on his forearms.

She realized with a shock that they had only kissed once.

It seemed a terrible oversight. They ought to have kissed a thousand times by now. But he wasn't kissing her; he was untying her. It felt equally intimate in her mind. He moved next to the ties at her ankles and had to use his teeth to get those undone. It was playtime suddenly as he chewed at the fabric scraps, leering at her, then biting her calf.

She laughed and squirmed, feeling totally new. It was like he untied her from the old Wednesday, from her old life that had tethered her to some dark space. Fun in bed, what a novel occurrence. She'd never laughed in bed with Vincent, not once in five years. She'd cried and come for him, but laughed like this and played?

Daniel crawled up her body to untie her other wrist. He looked down at her while he worked at the knot with his hands. She shivered from the look he gave her, and the strong, unfamiliar feelings in her heart. Warning bells were going off. *You're falling in love already, Wednesday. You're falling in love.*

But Daniel had given her no ultimatum about not loving him. He actually wanted them to be lovers—true lovers, romantic and sweet. He didn't understand that Wednesday was afraid to fall in love, and she didn't want to tell him. He would think she was weird. She *was* weird. She was terrified of loving, of needing someone. She'd seen what love did to her father. After her mother died, he was never the same. Then there was the way Vincent had crushed her when he left her.

"What? What's wrong?" he asked as he undid the last tie and set it aside.

"Nothing." *I'm just freaked half out of my mind right now.*

"I'll buy you new sheets tomorrow, I promise. I'll send them over."

She laughed. "No, it's not the sheets. I have plenty of those."

"What, then? Tell me."

She thought a minute, framing protests and confessions. *Don't expect me to love you. Can't we slow things down? God, help me.* In the end she said, "Would you like to spend the night?"

His smile was blinding.

God, help me. Please.

* * *

When Wednesday woke, morning light was filtering into the room. Daniel stirred beside her, reaching out to enfold her in his arms. It was an unfamiliar feeling, this morning coziness. Vincent had usually woken her with a thrust of his cock. But Daniel turned her to him and kissed her, and stroked her arms.

She sighed and stretched as he nuzzled her. Why did he have to feel so right? These sudden new feelings of contentment scared her more than anything he could do to her with his belt. His lips traced lower, to the tops of her breasts, then he took one nipple in his mouth. She pressed closer to him, overcome with desire and unfamiliar emotions.

"Mmm. You like that." It wasn't a question.

She moaned as he took the other hard peak in his mouth. She couldn't have spoken if she'd tried, even if he'd ordered her to.

"Give me your hands," he said. "Moan again for me."

It was impossible not to. She moaned and sighed and gasped for him as he held her hands hard. Soon he was using his teeth, gently nipping and biting her nipples, first one and then the other. Each wicked pluck and nibble made her clit ache harder. He pulled her hands up over her head and rolled on top of her. She felt pinned and helpless—her favorite feeling. Her pussy grew wet and hot for him. "Daniel..." She was begging. She wanted him more than anything on earth, but he merely looked back at her with a lazy smile.

"Soon. Be patient. When I'm ready."

She moaned even louder. He let go of her hands, and she flailed for purchase as his fingers infiltrated the hot, slick channel between her thighs. She bucked against his hand, desperate to draw him closer. Deft fingertips played over her pussy in a silky, slow cadence, melting her, subjugating her senses. She touched his hair, gingerly at first, then boldly, squeezing the golden-blond strands in rhythm with the song he was playing against her clit.

"Okay now." He stroked her, making her shiver. "Be a good girl."

Yes, yes, I'll be good as gold if you'll just stop teasing and fuck me.

Finally he left her to get a condom and stood over her, rolling it on, wearing a look she couldn't place. Desire? Mastery? Infatuation? She wanted him to take her, and take her hard. He climbed onto the bed and thrust her legs open with his powerful thighs. He lay on top of her and pulled her hard against him, skin to skin.

"I've got you, Wednesday. Don't I?"

"Yes, Sir," she whispered.

His body fit against hers like a puzzle piece. She basked in the feel of his hard muscles, his rough chest hair against her nipples. She scratched at his back and his taut buttocks, digging her nails into the landscape of his body. He growled against the side of her neck.

"Behave. Be patient. You'll get the cock. I know this isn't how you were taught."

She stilled at those words. No, this wasn't at all what he'd taught her. This was something else altogether. Daniel's lovemaking was so different from what she'd experienced with Vincent. Daniel made her feel like she was floating, even when he was holding her down. He made her whole body vibrate from the confidence of his touch.

Daniel parted her legs wide, lifted her hips, and plunged inside. She squeezed him tight, her nerves singing from the bliss of his cock stretching her. He fucked her, pressing down against her so she couldn't breathe, couldn't move without his yielding space and breath to her. Each time he moved inside her, she felt a strong sensation of being one with another person. With him. It amazed and terrified her, and she tried to shrink away.

"No," he said in her ear. "Don't."

She clung to him, pressing so close that she felt his pubic bone rubbing against her clit. It was a hard, stimulating resonance against her softness. He took without apology, but he brought her with him, urging her to active participation in their dance. It scared her, the impulses and desires he elicited in her. It scared her how hot he made her burn.

"Daniel, Daniel, I need..." What did she need? With Vincent, it had never been about her.

"What?" he asked. "What is it?"

"Daniel, can I come now, please? Am I allowed?"

He chuckled. "With or without my permission, I think you will."

He was right—either way it was going to happen. She would take a hundred lashes to feel the pleasure he was giving her now, to give in to the climax that was threatening to overwhelm her.

"Come," he said, "and do it like you mean it."

She orgasmed a moment later, with stars behind her eyelids and her blood beating in her ears. Each pulse and undulation of her climax seemed to take her whole body and shake it loose. Loose from fear. Loose from emptiness. When she regained her senses, he was looking down at her strangely, and she realized she was crying. Not a tear or two from the power of the orgasm. No, she was sobbing. She put her hands to her cheeks, and they came away soaked with tears. She stared at them, stupefied.

"I don't know—I don't know why…"

"It's okay."

The tears weren't stopping. She closed her eyes, embarrassed.

"No, open," he said in a low voice.

She opened them and shook her head. "I can't explain—"

"That's okay. You don't have to. I want you to look at me though, to see me. To know that I'm the one who moved you this way."

It was almost painfully difficult for her, but she kept her eyes on his as he wished.

He tilted his head. "Are you hurt? Did I hurt you?"

No. It's just that I've never felt this way before. Her breath caught, and he rolled away.

"I suppose you could use some air."

He didn't leave her, only lay beside her with his arm across her waist. He was so possessive. She both loved it and hated it. She was relieved to have his weight off her, but also anxious to have it back. He gave a contented sigh, turning onto his back.

"I really enjoy fucking you, Wednesday. I really do."

She was silent. To her, what he'd done was more than fucking. It was ecstasy. Ruin.

"Maybe," he said, looking over at her with a thoughtful expression, "maybe I'll fall in love with you and marry you, and we'll live happily ever after."

She made a strangled sound. "I don't know. This isn't a fairy tale."

"Isn't it? You're not a princess, and I'm not your prince?"

"I don't know yet."

He sighed and sat up on the side of her bed. "I don't want to go. I don't want you to disappear on me."

"Disappear? You know where I work."

"I want to have times, regular times, to see you. Nights that are mine, that I can look forward to."

The softness was gone. He was giving orders. She sighed, watching him stand and move away from her. "I can't do that," she said. "Not yet."

He scowled at her as he dressed. "Why the hell not?"

She toyed with the shreds of sheets next to her. She was untied, free, but for how long? Not long at all, it seemed, if he had his way. His eyes were stormy, and his mouth was set in a stubborn line. She wasn't free at all, and it grated on her suddenly.

"Can I just call you?"

"No. I want to set something up now. Dinner, movie, whatever you want. How about Wednesday, Wednesday?"

"Wednesday is okay with me. Dinner...I guess...if you want."

"Yes, I want," he said. "I'll pick you up at seven. Don't wear any panties under your dress."

5   CHAPTER FIVE

It was six thirty on Wednesday night, and Wednesday was preparing herself to see her lover. She'd plucked, waxed, soaked, showered, and perfumed her body to his standing specifications. Then she put on the lingerie, sheer and sleek. The push-up bra, the stockings, but no panties, not tonight. She would need a dress, though, for dinner with Daniel. She chose the style of dress he seemed to like best—sweet and provocative in an innocent-schoolgirl kind of way.

The more things changed, the more they stayed the same. Her slow preparations felt warm and familiar, like putting on a favorite coat finally back in season. As she sat to apply her makeup, her mind wandered in endless circles around Daniel, always Daniel. He'd called her earlier to remind her he would be picking her up at seven, as if she could possibly have forgotten. She had thought of little else, honestly, since he'd left on Sunday. Had she wanted time away from him to think? She'd had enough time. She wanted him now.

His voice on the phone had set her trembling, so deep and resonant, so firm. "Have you been a good girl since I saw you last?"

"I've tried to be, Daniel. But I've probably been a bit naughty."

He had laughed then, and there had been promise and fondness in that laugh. Vincent had laughed at her on many occasions, but not very often in a nice way, more often in a way that was cruel. She had laughed, truly laughed, with Daniel many times already, and she smiled even now, waiting for his knock.

He arrived right on time, him and his impeccable manners. As she undid the chain and lock, she remembered standing there, pressed against the wall, his hands all over her. He'd controlled her, taken her. Made her his. He'd done it right there beside the door less than a week ago. She tried not to look too giddy when she opened the door. Her heart hammered from the way he looked at her.

God, he was as gorgeous as ever, dressed in slacks and a gray cashmere sweater she wanted to rub against like a cat, in no small measure because it was tight enough to show off his muscles. His muscles, God. His arms, his shoulders, his rock-hard abs. She didn't dare look lower, lest she lose it completely.

Get a grip, Wednesday.

"Are you ready to go?" he asked, dragging his gaze from her décolletage.

"Yes." She wondered if later they'd go to his place or return here. One or the other—it really didn't matter to her as long as he was there.

He drove her across town to a wonderful, obscure jazz bar, and they fed each other tapas dishes over glass after glass of wine. She was no connoisseur of fine wine, not even close, but the wine he chose was absolutely delicious, and she drank probably more than she should have. She was flushed and excited, not just from the wine and ambience, but from the awareness of what was to come.

She was also aware of her nakedness under her dress. She kept her legs pressed together, but the way he looked at her made her feel exposed. They were both thinking about later, she supposed, but somehow they managed to talk like normal, civilized people over their meal. They talked about his work and hers, about their travels, their experiences, their likes and dislikes. They danced when she was nice and tipsy, and Daniel laughed as she tottered on her heels. Ever the gentleman, he held and guided her, compensating for her impaired balance. She laid her head on his shoulder, and he pulled her close. She drifted on the scent of him—clean soap or aftershave—and the warm, scratchy stubble against her cheek.

"You aren't going to sleep, are you?" he asked. "That's not allowed. Our night is just beginning."

"I'm not sleeping. I'm relaxing. You're so warm." She rubbed her cheek on his sweater as she'd ached to do all evening.

"You feel cold." He stroked her bare arm, giving her goose bumps. "I bet you're cold under your dress."

She laughed. "A little."

"Don't worry." He tightened his fingers on her waist. "I'll warm you up soon enough."

By the time they arrived at his house, she was a ball of impatient craving. He seemed equally worked up. He'd barely closed the door before his hands were up her dress. He cupped her ass, caressing it, and traced his fingers over the tops of her stockings.

"God. Down," he said.

"What?"

"Down, down on your back, now."

He pushed her to the floor and pulled her dress up so impatiently that she was glad it wasn't tight, because she had no doubt he would have ripped it to get at what was underneath.

He wrapped his arms around the tops of her thighs and parted her. She gasped as he kissed her pussy, licking and nibbling a trail to her clit. He was slow and deliberate, tasting her with broad, firm strokes and gentle teases. Daniel went down on her just as he had done everything else to her so far—with complete and utter abandon. Daniel exemplified unabashed carnal lust. Not mindless lust, though. No, he concentrated. Every moan, every movement she made caused some reaction in him. She imagined him cataloging her responses. *She likes that. She likes that. She doesn't like that quite so much. Ohh...that makes her moan.*

God. Oh...oh *God.* She bucked under him, her pussy flaring hotter and hotter, but he tightened his hold so she couldn't scoot away. He twisted his fingers in her garter straps as he kissed and sucked on her clit, worrying it between his teeth with just the right tension.

She had no idea what to do, whether to pull him closer or push him away. In the end she twisted her hands in his shag carpet to hold herself to the earth. Her pussy pulsed as he sucked her clit, then licked up both sides of her cleft. He prodded her with dexterous fingers, which were lubricated by the flood of her reaction. He finger-fucked and tongued her in a perfect symphony, and a climax twisted and built inside her. As she lifted her hips, arching for more contact, a leaf drifted to the floor beside her. She looked up in sudden confusion. Where was she, inside or outside? *Why is there a tree in his house?*

She was close, so close to orgasm. She reached blindly for him, and pulled roughly at his hair, something she would never in a thousand years have dared do to Vincent. It felt so soft and thick.

"God, please, Daniel... Don't stop!"

He didn't, only redoubled his efforts, pressing her clit with his tongue with exactly the pressure she liked. She took it as permission to go off whenever she wanted, and she did. She shuddered through wave after wave of blissful completion. She lay trembling afterward, unable to move, while he gazed at her with a self-satisfied grin. She stared back, totally speechless.

"You liked that," he said. "Good."

"Um, yeah. I definitely liked it. Daniel?"

"Yes?"

"Is there an actual *tree* in your house?"

"Yes, it's an actual tree. I'll tie you to it sometime."

She melted. "Oh yeah... I think I might like that."

"I'm quite sure you would."

"Can I ask you something else?"

"Anything."

She looked around the soaring, pristine walls and ceiling of the living room. "Why is your house so white? I've never seen a house like this. Without any color at all."

He grinned down at her. "You're the color."

"And you're a flirt." She laughed. "Really, though? Why all the white?"

He lay on his back beside her, looking up at the walls. "I don't know, Wed. I work in color all day. Busy film sets, lighting and shading. I want white at home. It's peaceful and pure. Plus...I don't know."

"What?"

"White walls are almost like a new canvas. I've always thought white was a color of...possibilities. What do you think?"

"I think white is a color of blandness." She tried to keep a straight face, but a string of giggles burst loose.

"I'll bland you, little lady," Daniel said, diving at her and tickling her.

She screeched, trying to fight him off. "Stop. Stop! Please, I hate being tickled."

"Hm." He regarded her with a raised brow and an "evil Dom" voice. "That's really good to know." He released her and stood. "Okay, my turn next. Dress off, stockings on. Let's go upstairs to my room."

He pulled her up and unzipped her dress before lifting it over her head and tossing it aside. He growled at the ensemble she'd worn for him. It was classic Hollywood slut wear: sheer push-up bra, high-waisted garter belt, and lace-top stockings in black. He made her walk in front of him up the stairs and down the hall to his bedroom, and he was awfully grabby for someone who was certainly, definitely about to get anything he wanted.

In his room, he ordered her to undress him, his face tense with lust and his eyes burning blue. A quick glance showed that his bedroom was as white as the rest of the house, except for the black wrought iron bed that dominated the space. It was artistic and ornate with lots of spindles for...

Well, Wednesday could guess what he needed them for. He might not have had a dungeon or a playroom like Vincent, but it would be no great thing for him to strap her to that massive bed a thousand different ways.

He seemed to have other plans. He sat on the edge of his bed and gazed at her with a look she was coming to know well. It was a look of *I want you, and I'm about to fucking take you. You'll do what I want, and you'll like it.* She stood as still as she was able to in her current state of arousal. She let him look at her, her chin up, her ass out, her arms at her side. The rug was shaggy, and she curled her toes in it.

"Turn around."

The way he said that had the power to drive her wild. She'd just come hugely, but that stern tone made her get all damp between the legs again. It was crazy the way he affected her. She showed him her back, and he drew in his breath.

"Beautiful," he said. "Let me see your hands, Wednesday. Put them at the small of your back."

She did and bowed her head. Time seemed to stand still, and she could feel his gaze like a caress roving over her back. Finally, she dared a look over her shoulder.

"Yes, okay. Come here. Stand in front of me."

She walked to him, met his gaze for a moment or two, but then her eyes were drawn to his cock. Every time she saw him erect, it gave her a jolt. He was definitely, *definitely* bigger than Vincent. Without a second thought, she started to drop to her knees.

"No." He pulled her up, then had her sidle even closer to him, between his legs. His cock was sticking up in front of her, poking at the juncture of her thighs.

"Look at me, Wednesday. Focus."

She blushed and tried to pull back, away from the huge distraction in front of her, but he held her fast with his hands planted on the globes of her ass.

"Do you know what I want to do to you?"

"Um...I have an idea."

"Don't be a smart aleck." His hands explored her where they willed, his fingertips ending up over the laces at the front of her garter belt. "This little outfit you had on under your dress all night— garters, stockings, no panties. I think you wore this just to provoke me."

"Um, you specifically told me not to wear panties."

He pinched the top of her thigh, below her ass. "I don't handle brattiness well at all." It was a warning, and she got it. *Don't be a smart aleck. Check.* His gaze traveled to her very erect nipples, which were clearly visible through her sheer bra, and back again to her face. "Perhaps you need to be whipped back into shape."

Whipped? Yes. She was finding it hard to breathe under his stare.

"Well," he said with a sigh. "I'll punish you later. First things first." He went to the nightstand for a condom and returned to sit on the bed. "Kneel in front of me and put your hands in your lap and act like a good girl, even if you're not."

She knelt and did as he ordered. Her gaze went from his face to his cock and back again. She wasn't sure where to look. It was pretty difficult not to stare at his cock when it was right in front of her like that. As he went on with his lecture, she started to realize that was probably his intention.

"I know Vincent kept you on your knees a lot, Wednesday. I understand that, but with me you won't just be dropping to your knees right and left. When I want you to kneel and suck me, I'll tell you to. The rest of the time, you'll wait for commands."

"Yes, Daniel." *New Master, new rules. Don't kneel until ordered to. Check.*

"Open your mouth." He drew her gaze back to his with two fingers placed beneath her chin. She parted her lips, feeling vulnerable and very, very hot. She felt terribly exposed looking up at him like that, her mouth open for him to use. She waited for him, at his mercy, at his behest, ready to service him on a word.

He didn't give orders right away, though, only traced the satiny head of his cock over her lips, over the tip of her tongue. It was an unexpected, erotic thing for him to do, and her body reacted, warm lust spreading and swirling. She was actually starting to salivate, anxious to taste him and take him in her mouth. He teased her. He controlled her. It was the control that made her burn hotter than anything else. He made her wait, and so she waited with her hands obediently folded in her lap.

"That's a good girl." The approval in his voice was like honey. "Don't take your eyes off me yet." He put on the condom, taking his time, smoothing it against his rigid flesh. Then he pressed her lips farther apart with his thumb and started to ease himself into her mouth.

"That's right," he whispered. "Good girl. You suck me now and make me come."

There was no possibility of a *yes, Daniel* at that point, since he was buried in the back of her throat, but she had every intention of doing exactly what he asked. Released from the excruciatingly intimate eye contact, she set out to blow his mind. With his size, it was hard to take as much of him as he wanted her to, but he was patient, letting her adjust to his needs. She slid her tongue across the latex barrier between them, hating it for separating her from his flesh. She wanted to taste every contour and trace every vein with the tip of her tongue. She loved the fullness of his rod, and she couldn't help but remember how it felt inside her—memories that triggered a hot rush of wetness between her legs. *Focus. Concentrate. Serve him.*

She found it awkward not to use her hands, but he'd told her to keep them in her lap, and he seemed pretty keen on easing in and out of her mouth himself, at his own teasing tempo. Still, she'd honed this skill for five years, so she only gagged a couple of times.

It wasn't long before his thrusts grew jerkier and more staccato. She worked him with her lips and tongue, savoring and teasing, then licking in broad strokes. With a raspy sigh, he told her to use her hands to fondle his balls. She did, weighing and caressing them, feeling them draw up with his peaking arousal.

He buried his fingers in her hair and pushed deep inside. She gagged again, but she doubted he even noticed at that point. Moments later, he climaxed with a stifled groan. She took the deep, finishing thrust, holding still with his balls cupped in her hand. She felt humbled and submissive to him, and waited to let him withdraw when he wished.

"Wednesday..." He sighed when he finally pulled away. He stroked her hair, then tilted her chin up so she stared into his eyes. "You're good at that. You've made me a very happy man."

"Happy enough to forgive me for being bratty earlier?" She only asked a question like that to reassure herself he would be strict with her.

"Lie down in the middle of the bed," he said softly. "Facedown."

Yes, he would be strict. She had known it all along.

* * *

Oh God. Beautiful. Beautiful. Beautiful.

Daniel was aware he was a very kinky man. That was never more apparent to him than at times like these, when something as basic as a woman lying facedown in the middle of his bed could make him lose his mind. The way she looked there, waiting for him, waiting for punishment... She had an amazing ass; she really did. The sexy bra, the lingerie, the black garter straps on pale skin—they were only the icing. Very nice icing, but even without it, her body was obscene.

He waited a long time, just watching, thinking about how to punish her. She'd been mouthy because she wanted to be punished, and he intended to show her how those types of games played out. He wanted to feel her against him this time, feel every fidget, every flinch. Every squelched impulse to flee. He wanted to feel her tense and uncoil as he spanked her. He wanted to feel her soft skin under his hand.

"Wednesday." She didn't look at him, only burrowed her face more deeply into the bed. "Wednesday," he said a bit more sharply. "Look at me when I talk to you."

"I'm sorry, Sir," she said, turning to peer up at him. She had quite a blush going on.

He sat beside her and stroked her hair. "Let me guess. You weren't allowed to look at Vincent when you were being punished."

"No. I wasn't supposed to."

"I want you to look at me always. I want to see you. Never more than when I'm punishing you. How else will I know how you feel?"

She was silent a moment. "Vincent never cared how I felt."

"Perhaps so, but I do." He took her arm and pulled her to him. "Come. Come here." He made her sit on his lap, a little bundle of trembling loveliness. "Look at me."

She swallowed and met his eyes. He ran his fingers over the tops of her stockings.

"I'm going to spank you first, and it's going to hurt, but if you're good for that, then I'll fuck you and let you come. Okay?"

"Okay. I'll try to be good. But...how hard will you spank me?"

"Pretty hard. Very hard actually. Harder than last time."

She drew a deep breath. "Okay."

"What's the matter? Are you afraid? Or are you excited?"

She shook her head, and her black ringlets tickled his cheek. "I don't know. Both."

"Okay, then," he said. "Over my lap."

It was so intimate, her capitulation, the way she draped her body across his thighs. He pretended to help her, to position her, but she knew exactly how he wanted her. Head down, ass up, hip barely grazing his cock. *Oh God. Beautiful.*

He caressed her upturned bottom, lustfully, yes, but gratefully as well. She was his. She was giving herself over to him. He let himself have a growl over it. As if in answer, she squirmed, wiggling her bottom. Her hip bumped his cock, arousing new frissons of craving.

He brought his hand down on her ass, a nice, hot crack to get things started. She jumped in his lap. He took his time, warming her up a bit before he fully lit into her. She was so lovely, tensing and struggling to be still, taking the pain only to please him. Even though she'd already sucked him off, his cock pulsed to life again. When he began to spank her harder, she cried out and reached back to cover herself. Her breath was coming in gasps, but he knew she wasn't to her limit yet.

"No," he said. "You know better."

"You're hurting me. It really hurts!"

"It's supposed to hurt. It's a spanking."

She moaned, pressing her cheek against his leg.

"Please, I've learned my lesson. I won't be bratty again. Please, I'll do anything. I'll suck you again, even better this time."

"Did bargaining work with Vincent?"

She visibly deflated. "No, Sir."

"It won't work with me either. Give me your hand. I'll help you keep it out of the way if you don't have the discipline to do it yourself." He took her hand in his and drew her arm up across her back. He wasn't that angry about her little bargaining attempt. He'd expected it. She would try all kinds of stuff in the beginning to see if he'd let her get away with it. She would learn quickly that he wouldn't.

He started to spank her again, trying to focus on the task at hand and not her shapely, reddening bottom. She struggled and fought against him when the pain was hard for her to take. Her fist clenched and unclenched in his grip as he belabored her bottom until his hand stung. She finally started to cry, just small, shaky sobs, but they were so damn endearing. He gave her a good volley of smacks to finish her off, and the music of her sobs rose to a wail.

"Okay, that's all for now." He pulled her up into his arms and kissed her tears. "You're my good girl, aren't you? You took that very well."

"I...I tried to, Daniel. But it hurt."

"Yes, it tends to. It didn't hurt that much, though. I think you're just a crier sometimes."

"It hurt a lot."

"Well, you know why it hurts, don't you? Why I hurt you?"

She buried her face against his neck. He felt her shudder, felt the renewed gush of her tears. It seemed so intimate, her hot tears against his skin. "I...I think I know why. Because you care about me?"

No. Because I'm falling in love with you. "Yes, because I care about you very much, and I want you to know that and remember it later when I'm not around."

She shifted on his lap. "I don't think that will be a problem."

She looked down, noticing what he was already well aware of—his endless erection rising again. He tossed her back on the bed and turned her roughly onto her tummy. God, that beautiful ass. He took the time to kiss each reddened cheek before he reached for a condom and nestled between her legs. He slid one hand down her front to find her mons and part her gently. She was so wet for him. He tormented her, tracing her most sensitive spots only to feel her vibrate with need. "You're mine, aren't you? You're really mine."

"Yes, Daniel." She squirmed under his touch, moving her ass back against him.

"No, wait. I know you want it. Be patient."

He smiled at her plaintive moan and teased her some more, just for fun. He took his time stroking her, trailing his fingertips through her swollen, soaked pussy lips. Her breath grew more and more erratic under his chest. He dipped his cock inside her from behind, just enough to addle her. It took every bit of his control not to thrust in her to the hilt. He pulled back, enjoying her soft, hapless sounds of disappointment.

"Daniel! My God!"

"No, not yet." He teased her again, entering, then backing out. She writhed under him, bucking against him when he drew away.

"Please!"

"Does it feel that good, Wednesday? Have you no self-control?"

"No! Damn! No, I don't." She made an amusing attempt at modulating her voice. "No, Sir, I don't— I can't— Please, Daniel, please—"

"Please, what? Say it. Beg me. '*I want you to fuck me.*'"

"God, please, I want you!"

"'*Daniel, I want you to fuck me.*'" He teased her again with the tip of his cock.

"Daniel, I want you to fuck me!"

He twisted his fingers in her hair and pulled her head back to his. "Will you be a good girl if I give you what you want? Will you behave?"

"Yes yes yes!" She twisted under him.

"Stop fidgeting," he said. "Don't be naughty."

She fell still, breathless, waiting.

"Good girl." He entered her slowly, a half inch, an inch at a time, until he was completely seated. Her warm pussy gripped him, massaging his aching length. He wanted the acute sensation to last forever. "Just let me fuck you. Let me go deep, let me feel you."

She made a groany-sobby sound as he held her and eased steadily in and out. He looked down at her tight, round ass and almost lost it.

"Daniel!"

"Shhh. You wait for me." He fingered her clit, stroking it in rhythm with his deep thrusts. "No, don't come yet. Not yet." He was having a hard time drawing their sexual encounter out, but she seemed to have it worse. She was actually holding her breath. He supposed it was cruel to hold her back that way. She must have had some special gift of nerves or anatomy that made it impossible for her not to orgasm with clitoral stimulation. But she tried, she tried so hard, and it touched him how she tried.

"Okay," he said. "Soon. Don't pass out now."

He never wanted to stop. He never wanted to stop fucking her. He traced up the curve of her hip to the small of her back, then up to her nipples, which were hard as little stones. He pinched one and was rewarded with a throaty moan and renewed begging.

"God, oh God, please!"

"Okay." He sighed, feigning impatience. "Come if you must, you ridiculous girl."

She went absolutely wild, and he loved every second of it. The snapping of her hips and her openmouthed gasps tipped him over the edge, and he came too in a devastating pulse and explosion, bucking inside her. They lay together afterward, an exhausted heap, his front to her back, his fingers fisted in her hair. She smelled like sex and sugar. She was hot like fire against him. He turned her head to him and kissed her again and again, deeper and deeper, drinking her in like wine. He kissed her until she could barely breathe, just to feel her gasp and come up for air.

6 CHAPTER SIX

Daniel had work to do, but he couldn't concentrate. She haunted him every fucking minute of every day. He had set plans to prep, real work to accomplish, but all he could think of was Wednesday. Thank God he was seeing her tonight. It had been a long three days.

Three days.

Three days and he was just about driven to madness. Pathetic.

Okay. He was going to call her. He would talk to her a while, then he'd buckle down, get his work done before their date. He had to call her anyway to see if she'd gotten his gift. He put his hand on the phone, but it rang as soon as he touched it. Maybe it was Wednesday calling. He looked down at the display. Fuck.

"Hello," he said tightly.

"Daniel. How are you?"

"I'm fine. And you?"

"I'm doing great. How is our Wednesday?"

Our Wednesday? I don't think so, you old lecher. He bit his tongue, hard. Vincent had passed her on to him, which he supposed deserved some gratitude and some limited polite conversation, however insincere. Hell, Vincent probably hated him every bit as much as he hated Vincent.

"So," Daniel asked, "what do you want?"

"You promised to keep in touch with me. That was one of the terms of our deal, was it not?"

"Listen, I'm not one of your shrinking subs, so I'd appreciate you not taking that tone with me."

"Did we or did we not agree you would keep me apprised of Wednesday's well-being?"

"Fine," Daniel said through gritted teeth. "What would you like to know?"

"She's with you now?"

"Yes, we're dating. I'm seeing her tonight for the third time."

"Only the third time?"

"We only went out for the first time last week."

"What took you so long?"

"Look who's talking! Could you have taken any longer to break up with her? Look, she's fine. She's doing great. We're getting along fine so far."

There was a long silence from Vincent's end, then a frustrated sigh.

"That's all you'll give me? That's it?"

This whole conversation, this whole situation made Daniel's skin crawl. This was what he got for entering into an unholy alliance with a twisted old pervert. The only reason, the *only* reason he'd agreed to play along was because he knew Vincent had truly loved her and probably loved her still.

But God, he really had to play along. Vincent had him over a barrel now, because if Wednesday found out how Vincent had plotted to pass her off to Daniel so he could let her go and still keep tabs...

"Listen, things are going well. We're making progress. But as I said, tonight will only be our third official date."

"You'll have to press her to get her to come to you. She tends to hide."

"I've seen that. But she's doing okay. I'm taking things slowly. I don't want to scare her off."

"Of course," said Vincent, and the way he said it, it sounded like *you're an ass.*

"Anyway, I've got to go. I was about to call her."

"What are you doing tonight? Taking her out?"

"Yes, out to dinner. I take her out on dates, you know, treat her like an actual woman. She's finally getting used to it, although it was alien to her at first." Daniel was unable to curb the self-righteous sarcasm from his voice.

Vincent chuckled. "Good. I'm glad to hear it. She was always a quick learner. Very quick. I knew she'd be all right, and as you know, I wish both of you only the best."

"Thank you." *Go to hell, you fucking bastard.*

"I'll talk to you later, then. Enjoy yourself tonight. Give her some good licks for me."

Ugh. Daniel felt so dirty after that conversation that he had to take a shower before he could talk to her. He dressed and looked at his watch. It was just after four o'clock. She should have gotten his package by now. She picked up on the third ring, her lovely, shy voice in his ear.

"Hello?"

"Hello, sweet."

"I think I will look sweet in these white, lacy things you sent."

"Hmm. White probably isn't your color, but we can pretend."

"Possibilities," she said jauntily.

He wanted to jump through the phone and have her right then. Instead he said, "Yes, possibilities. I'm sure you'll look lovely in it. I can't wait to see you tonight. Did you find the other things?"

Yesterday he had gone shopping for her and had the things wrapped in a white box with a pretty white bow. A white lace bra and a hopelessly frilly white garter belt, white back-seamed stockings made of real silk, and at the bottom of the box, white fur-lined cuffs that would be soft as a cloud against her skin.

She sighed. "Yes, I found them, Daniel. Thank God my sheets are safe."

He laughed. "Yes, your unfortunate sheets."

"Should I wear the cuffs too, with everything else?"

"Oh, you'll wear them—and very often, but leave them off for dinner, or the people in the restaurant might stare."

"You're probably right. They're so beautiful, though. Where did you find them?"

"I know a lady who makes them. I've already ordered a matching set in black." And burgundy and gold and green and lavender. "You don't worry about where I got them, little one. You just be sure you bring them along tonight."

"Yes, Daniel," she said in that way that made him wild with lust.

"I'll pick you up at seven sharp. I'm dying to see you."

"I'm dying to see you too. Where are we going?"

"Somewhere nice," he said.

"Very nice?"

"Yes, somewhere really very exceptionally nice. It'd better be, considering what I plan to do to you later."

He could almost hear her squirm through the phone, that subtle change in her breath.

"Seven o'clock, Wednesday. Be ready for me."

* * *

Wednesday watched him from across the living room. The way he stared at her... Between them, the tree rose out of the floor from somewhere beneath the foundation. When it was really quiet and the air conditioner blew, she could hear the faintest sound of rustling leaves. She'd had some vivid fantasies about the tree since she'd met Daniel. She had a strong feeling some of them were about to be fulfilled.

They'd rushed through dinner, barely taking stock of the sumptuous restaurant and gourmet fare. He'd driven her to his home quickly afterward. Now she stood near the tree with the white soaring walls above her, feeling pinned like a butterfly by his gaze.

"Undress," he said. He was still in a shirt and tie and pants with perfect creases. He watched, unmoving, as she kicked off her shoes and set them aside. She undressed as slowly and sensually as she could, down to the white lingerie he'd given her.

She looked up at him. "Take off everything?"

His lips curved. "Not everything. You can stop there."

She touched and admired the lingerie, partly to arouse him, but partly because it was so thrilling to be dressed in his gift.

"Thank you for these beautiful things. I love to wear them. They're the next best thing to having your hands on me."

"You're welcome. It's my pleasure. Literally." He laughed, but the smile didn't touch his eyes. He just stared, stared, stared at her until she shivered.

"What are you thinking?" she finally asked.

"I'm trying to decide what I'm going to do to you once I get you tied to that tree."

Her gaze flicked to the solid trunk, the leafy lower branches. "Do I have any say?"

"Absolutely not. But I'm sure you'll enjoy whatever I dream up."

She gave a come-hither smile and tried to look as enticing as possible, trailing her fingers absently over the tops of her thighs. He studied her with a half smirk as if to say, *I know your tricks.* A moment later he started to undress with an air of intent.

"You've decided on a plan of action?" She watched his beautiful body as it was revealed to her. Golden, muscular male. She loved the shift of his buttocks when he kicked his pants off and the ripple of his back when he bent to take off his socks.

"Yes, I have. I've decided I'm going to fuck you until you beg for mercy. I'm going to fuck you so much that you're just not going to feel right unless my cock's inside you. Bring me the restraints, Wednesday. The ones I bought you."

He didn't have to ask her twice. She dug them out of her bag, suddenly shy, and went to stand in front of him, placing them in his outstretched hand.

He closed rough fingers around the cuffs, and caught her elbow with the other hand, pulling her close.

"My little doll. You look like a doll, dressed up like this."

"I never had any dolls that dressed like this."

"Didn't you? I would have thought you sprang right from your mother's womb in fishnets, holding out a whip. Give me your hands."

A shadow crossed her mind, some distant thought, but she pushed it away. She held out her hands, and he fixed the cuffs on to her wrists. The fur was soft against her skin, but the leather outer part was strong and unyielding. She shivered, stealing a glance at his face.

His lips were so beautiful, pursed in concentration. He lifted his gaze to hers, piercing blue eyes through bronze-blond lashes. He raised her hand to his lips and kissed the inside of her wrist just beside the leather. He kissed the other wrist, and then he kissed her on the mouth, holding the cuffs' attachment points hard. His lips were warm and rough, his tongue invasive. He bent her head back with the force of his kiss.

"Daniel," she whispered when they parted. She sought him with her fingertips, but the cuffs held her fast, controlled by his hand.

"Go stand by the tree."

He gave her a push in the right direction, which was just as well, because his kiss had pretty much shut down her brain activity. She went to the tree, and he followed. He pressed her forward against the peeling white bark. He lifted her arms, and she looked up to find a hook fixed into the tree, camouflaged by the base of a branch. There was also a chain with clips on it. He hooked her cuffs to different links until he found the one where she barely had to go up on her toes. She tested the strength of her bonds, tugging on the chain. She felt a rushing flood of heat to her pussy as she realized she couldn't get away.

The restraints weren't big, but they had hook-and-loop closures that didn't give at all, and the chain was steel solid. He watched her pull and twist, an avid spectator. Again with the stare, and now she was doubly pinned, by his gaze and by the cuffs, which allowed her to turn but not get away. He put his hands on her waist, turning her outward. The bark scratched against her ass. She didn't want to snag her garter belt, so she went still. His gaze roved over every inch of her.

"What are you doing?" she whispered.

"Looking at what's mine."

She swallowed hard and shifted. When he talked like that, it made something inside her melt into a puddle. *Please touch me.*

"I like you in white. You were made to wear white, a sweet girl like you." He ran his hand over her belly and down between her legs, a skilled, teasing trail. She arched her back, giving herself up to his talented touch.

He sank to his knees, his soft hair trailing down her center. She felt his palms between her legs, lifting her, parting her. He knelt and began to kiss her between her thighs. His hot breath whispered over her, and his stubble was a thrilling chafe against her skin. He went to work on her clit, tasting her like a starving man. His tongue flicked and lapped, every movement of his mouth a more insistent invasion. He squeezed her thighs where he held her parted and open to him. Her pelvis ached, and she started the slow, tense climb to orgasm.

"Oh Jesus! Oh God." She moaned, twisting her hips to feel more of the hot, wet bliss. She pulled at the bonds, spread her legs wider, then drew them together as much as she could, only to have him push them open again. His mouth was driving her crazy. She wondered briefly how many girls he must have been with to hone this kind of skill. *Don't think about it, Wednesday.* "God," she whispered. "Please don't stop. Ever!"

"I won't," he said against the inside of her thigh. "Not until you come."

It was a shamefully short time later that she did just that. She would have liked to draw it out, to have had him love her like this for hours, but her body betrayed her as always, and she couldn't make it five minutes against the talents of his mouth. Hot waves of release overtook her, and the tension snapped like a slingshot. Her nerves sang and her body shuddered until she came to rest, hanging from the restraints. He sat back when her noisy cries of satisfaction faded, a lascivious smirk on his face.

"You're a show-off," she said.

"Be careful, darling." He stood and pinched one of her erect nipples, sending a sharp aftershock to her clit. "Respect, please."

"Thank you, Sir. That was lovely."

"Better. You're welcome." He stared at her, stroking himself. He was hugely erect. He turned and left, leaving her swinging there like a prisoner in chains. Her legs were still shuddery from her orgasm, and she leaned against the tree, drawing deep breaths. He was back a moment later, rolling on a condom. "I'm going to fuck you now. Right there. Would you like that?"

She writhed in the restraints from the way he said it, all growly whisper. She nodded eagerly.

"Answer me out loud. Say it."

"God, I want you, Daniel. I really do."

He laughed. "You'll have to do better than that."

"Daniel, I want you to fuck me, please!"

"Hmm...that was slightly better. But I don't know."

"Daniel, please, please fuck me, I want your big, hard cock inside me now. Please!" She pulled at the restraints in earnest. He smiled.

"That was pretty good. I'm still not fully convinced, though." He ran his hands over her breasts, squeezing them painfully, then slid his palms lower, over her hips and behind her to cup her ass cheeks. He lifted her again, pinning her to the tree with his solid body. She clung to the cuffs, still affixed to the hook. Bark scratched between her shoulder blades as he ground against her front like some woodland satyr. She looked up into crisscrossing branches and delicate leaves as he entered her just a little. It was a teasing, hot press, the promise of satisfying penetration, but at her relieved moan, he drew out again.

"No, please, Daniel! Please don't tease me again."

It was so unfair. He just laughed and watched her squirm, caught by the restraints. She couldn't bring him closer, couldn't run her hands all over his body the way she wanted to. "I enjoy torturing you," he said. "Thought you might have figured that out by now."

"You're mean."

"Tone, Wednesday. Watch your tone. I believe I'm the one in charge here. Anyway, I've decided I'm going to birch your bottom first."

He let her down, turned her around in a very businesslike way, and reattached her cuffs to a higher link of the chain so she was definitely pulled onto her toes. "Don't go anywhere," he said with a smirk.

She turned her head and watched as he pulled down one of the lower branches. He twisted off a slender switch and stripped it of its leaves. She was scared—and she liked to be scared—but man, she was horny too. She was so aroused from what he'd done to her so far, and by his declaration that he was going to birch her...just because. Just because he had power over her. Just because she was under his control. Just because he wanted to. It pushed every button that made her who she was. Masochist, kinkster, pain slut. His. *Oh God, I love him.*

"Daniel, I...I—" She couldn't say it. She couldn't explain what she felt. She swallowed instead as he brandished the birch switch at his side, as if testing its capabilities. "I've...I've never been birched before. I'm kind of scared."

"That makes it even more fun for me."

She giggled softly, and then he thwacked the switch hard against the trunk just beside her. She jumped out of her skin. "Oh God, Daniel."

"Are we having fun yet?" He tapped her ass cheeks with it a couple of times. "Stick your ass out, Wednesday. So I can aim better."

"Hell no!"

"Do it." With a sigh, she arched her back for him and thrust her bottom out.

Thwack! The sizzle of fire burned in a stripe across her ass. Oh God, freaking... God... It fucking hurt. He rested the switch against his hand and sighed. "You're so beautiful, Wednesday. I could do this for hours. I really could."

"I'd rather you didn't." *Thwack!* Ow!

"Sarcasm, darling. Watch it."

Another cut of the switch lashed across her backside. She twisted sideways and tried fruitlessly to pull her hands away so she could cover herself. He only turned her back around and began again, delivering another stroke as she pulled and sobbed for respite. The pain was so brutal, yet so fulfilling.

She could see the hint of him in her peripheral vision. A whine rose in her throat, dread for the next blow, which fell without mercy, crisscrossing the other four strokes so her ass felt outlined in pain. She pressed her cheek to the scratchy bark, bracing for more, but not sure she could take more. Instead she felt the touch of warm fingertips, a soothing contrast to the fire of the lash. He tossed the switch to the floor and pressed against the back of her, burying his head against her hair.

"God, you get to me, Wednesday."

He turned her and kissed her deeply, twisting her nipples with a ruthless, painful tug. He lifted her hips in a bruising grip and thrust inside. She was pinned and powerless, subjugated by hot, rigid flesh. He slid out and in again, driving her thighs apart. She felt the drag of the restraints on her wrists, her shoulders. Her ass cheeks still stung from the switch; each stroke pressed her back against the tree, so she felt deliciously sore and fidgety.

"You like it? You like to feel my big cock fucking you?"

"Yes, Daniel! God, yes."

"Pounding into you? I should have birched you harder, but I couldn't wait to get inside your pussy, you hot little slut."

Dirty talk, but the words were like a caress. Sick, sexy stimulation applied directly to her brain stem via her naughtier parts. She ground her clit against his front. *Don't come. Don't come.* She didn't want the switch again, or maybe she did. She wanted whatever he gave her. She felt his mouth against her ear, a hot, wicked bite on her lobe. He slid his hands up to squeeze her breasts and pinch her nipples, sending craving tingles sliding into outright fire.

"I want to mark you, and I want to own you. I want to fucking live inside you." His words were a brand, resonating in her pussy as he drove her closer and closer to release and ecstasy. She clenched her thighs with longing, heat flaring through her entire center and up to her belly and breasts.

"Oh God, Daniel. Please, please, may I come, Sir?"

"Yes, girl. I want to feel it. I really want you to move."

The flame flared to a frightening crescendo. When the release came, it rolled in waves across her shuddering body. She kicked and bucked as sparks exploded in her pussy and clit, and her whole being seemed to contract around his cock. Her hair fell around her face in the midst of the wildness; she went positively feral. She was held fast by his body and by the bonds, by the towering tree, but at the same time she felt like she was flying. She threw her head back with a groan as the fire lulled to a shimmer, then sated exhaustion and ache. Her ass cheeks throbbed, and her pussy contracted around him in intermittent aftershocks. He came then, jerking up hard against her. She shivered as he traced his fingers over her straining arms.

"Untie me, Daniel," she said weakly.

"It's a little late now for safe words." He reached up and released her wrists with two *rrrrips*. She slumped down into his arms. He gathered her up and carried her over to his massive couch. He was a solid wall, supporting her. She was loose like a rag doll, too tranquil to do anything but breathe in time to his steady breaths. When he left to take off the condom, she felt bereft, abandoned. He returned in seconds, and they snuggled together on the velvet upholstery. He nibbled at her shoulder, slow, mild bites that soothed her. Every so often he ran his fingertips reverently across the rising welts on her ass.

"Wednesday," he said after a moment. "Why do you like it? Why do you like when I hurt you?"

She turned to him and reached her arms around his neck. She pressed her face to his damp skin, smelling aftershave and the scent of lingering sex. "You know, the hardest part of being in bondage is not being able to touch you."

"Don't change the subject. I'm curious. Why do you like when I hurt you?"

"I don't know," she said, drifting on the wonderful, manly smell of him. "I guess because I'm a masochist. And because afterward you're so awfully nice and you hold me and cuddle me and stuff."

"I would hold you and cuddle you without the other, you know."

She looked at him thoughtfully. "Why do you like to hurt me?" She wasn't sure how he would react to her turning the question back on him, but he shrugged and answered her quickly.

"Because it's beautiful how you submit to me. Because I love the way you react."

She trailed one finger down the side of his pensive face, feeling drowsier by the moment. "I like the way you react too. I like the way you pounce on me like you can't stand to wait another minute. I like everything about you. It's kind of amazing, really. Hey, can I sleep here tonight?"

"I would be disappointed if you didn't," he said. "But before you fall asleep on me, let's get you up into my bed."

7   Chapter Seven

He woke before her in the morning. She slept on beside him—a tired, cuddled-up girl in his bed. It didn't help that he'd gotten her up before sunrise to fuck her again. He slid out of the bed, trying not to jostle her, and pulled the covers around her before he tiptoed out of the room.

He started to do some work in his art studio, but found he couldn't concentrate with her so far away. He went back up to the bedroom and crawled in beside her with his laptop. He did good work for an hour, then put his laptop aside to gaze at her some more. She was so pale. Her skin was so beautiful and soft. She was so terribly, frighteningly vulnerable in sleep.

He looked at her long black eyelashes, which rested against her pale skin. She had dark smudges under her eyes that concerned him. Had he really worn her out so much? He would have to let her sleep and not molest her so much. He would try, anyway. He continued his silent perusal of her features. He was charmed to find a freckle or two on the bridge of her nose.

Those freckles, wow, so adorable. He just stared at them, picturing her as a child with that curly mop of black hair. It was always in the back of his mind that Wednesday had once been someone's daughter, someone's child. He felt he owed it to whoever had brought this beautiful Wednesday into the world to treat her fairly and responsibly, although it was difficult sometimes to picture a sex goddess like her as someone's child. Someone, sometime had wrapped her in a blanket to keep her warm, had cut the crusts from her sandwiches, had braided her hair, someone who had the same hopes and dreams for her that all parents did.

Or perhaps not. Vincent had told him she'd had a less-than-nurturing childhood. No mother to speak of, and a cold, emotionally distant father. It was easy to try to psychoanalyze, especially with the way she'd allowed Vincent to treat her. He couldn't imagine growing up without the loving warmth of a mother. His own mother still babied him, thirtysomething man that he was. He'd been an only child, like Wednesday, but he'd been spoiled rotten by two doting parents.

A rhyme he'd loved long ago came unbidden to his mind. He remembered his mother chanting it to him from his favorite book while she hugged him close.

Monday's child is fair of face,
Tuesday's child is full of grace,
Wednesday's child is full of woe,
Thursday's child has far to go.
Friday's child is loving and giving,

OWNING WEDNESDAY

Saturday's child works hard for his living,
And the child that is born on the Sabbath day
Is bonny and blithe and good and gay.

She'd been born on a Wednesday, surely, to have the name she did. He imagined her as a sad and serious child, sitting in a home devoid of any warmth. It wasn't difficult to see. *I like to just think about things sometimes for hours.* He wanted to squeeze her and hold her for a long, long time. He wanted to somehow make up for all that heartache. *Wednesday's child is full of woe.* How do you take away a childhood like that? With no one to nurture you, to make you feel valued and loved?

Daniel had been born on a Friday. He had plenty of love to give.

He sighed and gathered her next to him. He couldn't help it. If she woke, so be it. She stirred but didn't wake completely, content to sleep in his arms. He felt her heart beating against his chest. As much as it chagrined him, he realized now that Vincent had been right to pass her on to him. To not chance her falling into the wrong person's hands.

Anxiety seized him when he thought about losing her, thought of her being hurt in some circumstances beyond his control. *In turn, you'll keep me apprised of her well-being,* Vincent had said. *Or else I might lose my mind,* he'd probably added to himself. Daniel got it now, and he found some peace in that, but still, he knew Wednesday would never understand if she found out he was informing on her to Vincent.

She sighed in her sleep and whimpered softly. He pulled her closer. His Wednesday, lost and adrift in dreams. *Wake up.* He wanted to shake her from her cold, cold dreams. *You're with me now. Everything's all right.*

OWNING WEDNESDAY

* * *

They soon began seeing each other more often, sometimes several days a week, and at least once or twice a week she slept over, although at least as often she made excuses to go home. Sometimes they went out and did things together, but more often they stayed in and had sex, which they now did without condoms, since tests had been done and she was on the pill.

It pleased him inordinately to be her first—not the first one to have fucked her, but the first one to have fucked her skin to skin. The first time he'd slid inside her without the latex barrier between them, it seemed a metaphor for all the new closeness they felt. It was incredible, being able to feel her, really feel her, and she, who had never had sex without a condom, was absolutely dazzled. The entire time, she'd marveled at how different it felt.

To Daniel, it just felt very committed. That was the main reason he loved it so much. She wasn't crazy about taking the pill, but the alternative, getting pregnant, seemed to terrify her. She had grilled the doctor when they'd gone to get them. "Will these definitely work? You're absolutely sure?"

He'd given Daniel a strange look as she'd gone on and on. *Poor schmuck,* he'd probably thought, wondering why his woman was so dead set against having his child. Ah well, there were tons of things he didn't understand about Wednesday, but the pleasure of going bareback was more than worth the hassle of getting her on the pill.

Now that they were more settled as a couple, they tried to do things other normal couples did too. Sometimes they went to art shows or parties. He introduced her to some work friends, and she introduced him to some friends of hers. They were your average loved-up couple with a secret fantasy life that thrilled them both.

Vincent, unfortunately, continued to badger Daniel with phone calls, hounding him for information on how Wednesday was. Several times Daniel considered simply explaining all the machinations to her and hoping for the best. But in the end it seemed too risky, with the complicated way she felt about them both. He hoped eventually Vincent would get over her, and the whole secret deal would go away, but he was disabused of that notion soon enough.

Vincent became so persistent, Daniel began to worry she would be there with him sometime when he called. He finally agreed to meet with Vincent in person, and sneaked over to his house, looking over his shoulder. He knew Wednesday was at work, but still, he had an unreasonable fear of being caught. Daniel was only partly surprised to find a girl kneeling at Vincent's feet when he arrived.

"I'm training her for auction," Vincent said, between offering Daniel coffee and taking his coat.

"Yeah, okay." It was hard to keep the distaste from his voice. She was pretty, but she looked barely legal.

"She's a good girl, very talented. Would you like to try her out?"

"No."

"You're welcome to. I'm sure she'd enjoy it very much."

"She's lovely, Vincent," he said for her benefit. "But no."

"No, of course not. How silly of me." He patted the girl on the head, and Daniel saw Wednesday for a moment, kneeling there collared and cuffed. "Don't take it personally, Samantha. He's just very much in love with someone else. You *are* still in love with her, aren't you?"

Daniel shot him hostile look. "Of course I am."

"She's in love with you too?"

"I hope so. She says she is."

"And she's keeping herself up for you nicely?"

Daniel frowned. "What the hell kind of a question is that?"

Vincent looked surprised. "I certainly didn't mean to offend. She was always a very serious girl about her body, about her looks—"

"She looks fine. More beautiful than ever. It suits her, being with me."

"I'm sure it does. So, she's living with you now?"

"Not yet. Soon, I hope."

"You 'hope' she loves you. You 'hope' she'll move in soon. Who's the top here, you or Wednesday?"

What an asshole. How had she managed to put up with him for five years? The way Vincent spoke to him, it was as if he was asking, *Who's the top here, you or me?* Vincent clearly thought it was him.

"She's mine now," Daniel said, measure for measure. "What I hope for with her is none of your business."

"Isn't it? I suppose not. But I bet the sex is as good as ever. Have you been enjoying her? I hope you've been making good use of her ass."

"Vincent—"

"It's true she enjoys it probably more than a submissive should, but that doesn't mean you should deprive yourself. Not letting her come every once in a while worked wonders for me."

"Enough."

"What? You have to remember what she was to me. Just a sub. Not so sentimental a relationship as yours."

"You're so full of shit," Daniel said with a sharp laugh. "Why don't you cut out this posturing bullshit? Say what you really mean."

"What are talking about?"

"This isn't a game, you sick fuck. I'm not here to get you off. You sit there and ask me the stupidest questions. 'Does she still like to be ass-fucked? Does she still go to the gym?' Is that seriously all you want to know? Really? Don't you want to know if she's happy? Jesus, it's very disrespectful to her."

"I do not make a habit of respecting my submissives," Vincent said in a voice dripping with mockery.

Daniel narrowed his eyes and leaned forward, staring at him.

"I would like to hear, just once, how you truly felt about her."

"Daniel." Vincent tsk-tsked, as though he was the ridiculous one.

"No, I'd like to hear it from your lips. I'd like to hear you admit exactly how much you loved her, how much you still love her even now."

Vincent scowled.

"Samantha, go and wait for me in the bedroom. On your knees by the bed. Go."

"Yes, Master," she said, her eyes wide. No doubt she'd have preferred to stay and listen. She'd gotten an earful to think about. Daniel knew it was poor form to have spoken of such things in front of her, and Vincent was rightfully angry, but Daniel was tired of the way the man belittled Wednesday—especially when she had given him so much.

As soon as Samantha left the room on her hands and knees, Vincent glared at Daniel. "I'll thank you not to dress me down in front of any submissive of mine ever again."

"I'll thank you not to dress me down too, while we're asking. I'm not your toy. I'm not even your friend. I don't appreciate you using me to do this, to help you bust one more nut over your ex-sub."

"I gave her to you. A little gratitude might be called for."

"You have my gratitude, but you don't have my respect. I'm not going to share the details of our sex life with you, or the private parts of our lives. Ever. If you want to know how she's doing, if she's safe and happy, then fine, I'll share. Whatever else you want to know about her, you'll have to find out yourself. If she'll even speak to you."

After a moment, he sighed. "We're two very different people. We play this game differently."

"Yes, we do. And you'll remember that you chose me for her because of how I play."

Vincent rubbed his chin for a long time.

"That may be so. And it was because of how I play that I gave her up. I'll thank you to remember that before you exhort me again to confess my undying love for her." He stood. "Now, if you'll pardon me, I have some pressing work to get back to. Slavegirls can't train themselves. I'll show you to the door."

CHAPTER EIGHT

Wednesday was woken up on a Saturday morning in November by a delivery, a gift from Daniel. She slowly opened the box, then stifled a smile. As if she needed a reminder. Where the hell had he found a toy like this in pink? Daniel probably owned anal plugs in every color. She was already getting warm between the legs. There was a note.

I'll be there at seven. You'd better be wearing this.

She sighed and bit her lip. What a pervert he was. But yes, it would be her pleasure to wear it. Dinner...then dessert.

When he came to the door at seven, she was dressed and ready to go, and she had his toy in her ass as he'd ordered. He knew she did too, from the expression on his face. Instead of guiding her out the door, he pushed her inside. *Thank God*, she thought as his arms came around her. He kissed her, hard, deep, passionately, crushing her in his embrace. Then he drew up her dress and first found the toy, then the wetness between her thighs. He made a sound in his throat that scared her a little.

"Take your clothes off. Every fucking stitch."

She obeyed him as quickly as she could, before he started ripping stuff off the way he sometimes did. She took everything off, even her bra and stockings, until she stood before him completely naked, breathless, and flushed.

"I'm going to fuck you now, Wednesday. And as you probably suspect, it's not going to be in your hot little cunt."

She swallowed hard, feeling shivery as he too shucked his clothes. God, he was so hard already, his cock jutting out in front of him. She knew he wouldn't hurt her, but he looked like he absolutely could if he wanted to.

"Come here," he said, and guided her to the side of her bed. She felt vulnerable without the lingerie she usually wore. He bent her over, pushing down on her shoulders, and started to nudge her legs apart. She stiffened, but he said, "Wider. Open your legs for me now."

He took the toy out, and she heard the sound of a condom wrapper, then felt the cool lube against her ass. "I'm a big man, Wednesday," he said. "I'm going to need your cooperation. You're going to have to let me in."

"Yes, Daniel." *Yes yes yes.*

He paused and rubbed the small of her back. She was weak in the legs, remembering the first time he'd taken her ass, that night at Vincent's. That time she'd already been stretched by a larger toy than the pink one, and even then the toy had hurt quite a bit.

But she wanted it. She craved it, the conquering pain, only because it came at his hands.

"I've been dreaming of doing this to you all week." His rumbling voice vibrated against her shoulder.

"I've been dreaming of it too."

"Have you?" he said, pressing his cock to her tender hole so that she flinched a little. "You're not afraid, are you?"

"No, I'm not afraid."

"You want me? You want me to fuck your ass? What if I hurt you, baby?"

She moaned softly. "You can hurt me if you want."

He started to ease into her. God, his cock felt so huge. So frightening. So good. But then he pulled back out.

"God, please. Please!"

"Please what?" he asked. "Please fuck your ass?"

Oh Jesus, yes, please...

"Say it to me. Tell me what you want."

"Please, Daniel. Please fuck me."

"*'Daniel, fuck my ass.'*"

"Please, Daniel, fuck my ass. Please!"

She was pressing against the bed, trying to relieve the pressure in her clit, but he wouldn't let her. He drew her back against him with a low chuckle, teasing her with his cock. He was an absolute terror, and she was quickly losing it. If he didn't take her soon, after she'd dreamed of it all week... She'd dreamed of it for months, since that first night back in March. *Oh God...*

"Do you want me to spank you first?

"Oh God, Daniel." She buried her head in the bed and groaned in frustration. "This isn't funny."

"It's funny to me. I'll use my belt if you want. I know you like that."

She wiggled her ass back against his cock. "Please take my ass, Daniel. Please."

"Nice begging. Good girl. Arch your back." He ran his fingertips along her spine as she obeyed, opening to him. "Are you sure you're ready for me, Wednesday? Either way you're getting me. And you're going to stand there and take it like a good girl. You're not to pull away or move your hands from the bed, do you understand?"

"Yes, Sir," she whispered. "I'll be so good for you, I promise."

"You're going to open up and relax for me, like a good girl who wants to get her ass fucked."

He started to enter her again, just easing the head in. Oh Jesus. Wow, he was big. She breathed deeply, steeling herself against the burgeoning pain. It always ached at first, smarted like being pried open. She knew it would ease in a moment. He pressed into her slowly while she fidgeted and whimpered.

"Okay?" he asked.

In answer, she sighed and twitched her ass. Her body unwound and relaxed to accept the invasion. He grabbed her hips hard and groaned, moving deeper inside her.

"Oh fucking—God...you feel so good. I'm going to fuck you so hard, girl."

"Oh yes...please..." She remembered this feeling, this incredible, indescribable feeling of him taking and filling her ass, and she had not thought, months ago, that she would ever feel it again. She really, really loved ass fucking, preferred it, in fact, to regular intercourse. The edge of pain to it, the care he had to take, the intense feeling of sharing something so forbidden. For so long she had dreamed of and craved being taken this way.

He held her hips firmly to keep her skittering legs from collapsing. She grasped the comforter and lost herself in the deep humiliation, the deep surrender of giving up her most private place for his pleasure. He fucked her forever, taking his time, then picked up speed as his pleasure mounted.

"I love you like this, baby." He tightened his hands on her waist, holding her still, holding her trapped for him, just as he'd promised. Her clit throbbed and her nipples ached. She pinched them, trying to reach that summit building just beyond her reach. He noticed her squeezing her nipples and reached down and grasped them in a truly torturous grip. She cried out at the sharpening pain, throwing her head back. He pinched harder, harder still, until her nipples burned. She reached back to clutch his thighs, and he pressed her forward on the bed, driving into her with deep, urgent strokes.

"Come for me, baby. Come now. I want to feel you come with my cock in your ass."

More pain. Fingers ravaging her and his cock pinning her to the bed. He shuddered against her, awesome masculine power. "Come, damn you," he groaned as he bucked through his orgasm. His mastery, his sadistic tenderness all coalesced into a shattering climax that turned her inside out. She bit into the comforter as her whole pelvis clenched and contracted in a mind-bending squeeze. He hissed as she scratched him, and pressed harder into her ass. The orgasm peaked in a luscious vibration of contentment and left her breathless and limp.

After that they lay still together, her feet dangling off the floor. Every so often he moved in her, just resting in her ass. Finally he withdrew, turned her over, and kissed her, then nuzzled her jaw with his rough cheek.

OWNING WEDNESDAY

"Again," he said.

* * *

They never did get out to dinner that night, which was fine with Wednesday. They ended up at Daniel's house in his big whirlpool bathtub, eating takeout in the nude.

"I like this better," she said. "Better than going out with you."

"Do you? But I like to take you out. I like showing you off to everybody."

"I'm just as happy here. I like this, relaxing with you."

"Move in with me, then."

She choked on her lo mein.

"If you like this," he said, "move in with me. We could do this all the time. Every day. Every hour."

Wednesday held her tongue. There was nothing she could say that wouldn't sound mean. *All the time? I don't think I want you taking over my life. I don't want to always have you all over me, even though I like it once in a while.* She felt a sudden urge to run away from him, as far as she could go. Moving in? *Every day. Every hour.*

"The water's cold," she said. "I'm getting out."

He grabbed her ankle. His fingers felt like shackles.

"I'm cold, Daniel. Do you mind?"

"Yes, I mind. Why won't you even consider it?"

"I will consider it. Later. You want me to move in. I get it, okay? I don't feel like deciding right now. Is that okay with you, Master?" She said Master way too sarcastically, but her mouth was on overdrive. She yanked her leg again, trying to pull away, but he only tightened his grip. *Every day. Every hour.* Oh my God.

"Are you in a mood, Wednesday?"

"Maybe. Can't I be in a mood? Do I need permission from you now to be in a mood?"

"I think it's a little provocative when you're in a mood."

Her answer to that was to pull away even harder, but that only seemed to drive him on. He clamped his hand around her calf like a vise.

"I'll let go of your fucking leg when I'm good and ready, so you just simmer down and stand still."

She crossed her arms over her chest and stared at the wall until he finally released her. She didn't know why his offer angered her so much. She should want to move in with her lover, shouldn't she?

She wasn't really angry. She was afraid.

She lunged for a towel, wanting to cover herself, wanting to get away from him, but he was right behind her. She bolted, stalking into his bedroom while he followed on her heels. God, couldn't he see she needed some fucking space? When he reached for her again, she batted his hand away. "I wish you'd stop pawing at me all the time."

"I'll paw every fucking inch of your body," he said, pulling the towel away from her before she could think to grab it back. "And up inside it too if I want."

"You're so fucking crass. Give me the towel."

He was on her in an instant, pushing her back on the bed. She tried to squirm away. He was still wet, his dewy skin sliding across hers and his chest hair wet against her breasts. He tilted her chin up, but she stubbornly refused to meet his eyes.

"If you want to scrap, lover, we'll bypass the sex and go straight to the beatdown. Is that what you want?"

"No, that's what *you* want. I want to go home. I'm so fucking tired of your hands all over me. You're like some hyperactive, oversexed octopus!" she yelled in his face. She tried harder to get away from him, but the harder she tried, the more firmly he held her down. His mouth was set in a stubborn line. She wasn't going anywhere until he decided to let her.

"Shh, shh now." He used one hand to brush back an errant lock of her hair, the tender gesture at odds with the rough way he subdued her. "Settle down before you say something you're going to regret, baby."

"I'm not your baby," she said through clenched teeth.

"You're my baby."

"I am not!" He thought this was funny, but some guarded place in her heart felt threatened. "Let me go. I don't want to play these fucking games."

"I'm not into play, Wednesday. You know that."

"I'm serious. I'm not in the mood for this tonight. Don't you understand that?"

He was obscenely hard by this point. He pressed his raging erection against the juncture of her thighs, and she hated the surge of hotness that flooded her pussy.

"What are you in the mood for, then, lover?" His voice was a silken threat. He knew. Damn it. He knew that even now she wanted him, that he could take her and subdue her with just the authoritative tone of his voice. She tried to press her legs together, but he nudged them back apart.

"I think you're in the mood for a really degrading, nasty, cathartic fuck," he whispered. "The kind of fuck where you can't face yourself in the mirror afterward, but you feel a whole lot better."

"I am not!"

"I think you are, and I'm not too fond of the lying."

"I'm not lying. Let go of me."

"Shut your fucking mouth and spread your legs. Spread your legs wide open for me."

"No."

"Do it. Obey me."

She looked up at him finally, right into his eyes, and what she saw stilled her for a moment. Understanding wrapped in challenge, wrapped in love. She was burning up for him. She loved him. She hated him. It suddenly seemed important to fight him, to fight the part of herself that wanted what he offered.

He was her Dominant. She was his submissive. *I'm afraid. I'm afraid. I want you, but I'm afraid. Don't you see that?* She bared her teeth and narrowed her eyes. Fight or flight.

"If you want me to spread my legs, you're going to have to make me."

He made a guttural sound that almost made her fly right then and there. He started to tussle with her, but it was like a lion toying with a mouse. She put up a hard fight, but all he did was restrain her. She got her thighs locked together, though, no small victory, and she landed a few good slaps and one knee that came dangerously close to his jewels. He let her go at that point, and she took off. She heard him chuckle softly behind her. He thought he would have her. Maybe he would. Maybe she wanted him to.

She bolted down the hall to the spare room with him at her heels. She slammed the door and locked it a half second before he arrived. For a full minute she heard nothing but the rasp of her breath. *Every day. Every hour.*

"Wednesday, you have ten seconds to unlock this door before you get the thrashing of your life."

"Go away," she screamed at the barrier between them. He cursed once, then she heard only silence. Too late, she remembered the adjoining bathroom, which she hadn't thought to lock. She yelped as he descended on her and pinned her arms roughly behind her back.

"You never, ever run from me, do you understand? You never lock me out. Never."

She struggled to pull away from him. "You think you can have whatever you want, whenever you ask, at once. You think you own me."

"I do own you. That's not in question. You're mine like water is wet, you little fuck." He turned her, not letting go of her hands, and kissed her. She resisted, then she bit him. His controlled veneer snapped.

"I fucking warned you about the biting," he yelled, pushing her away. "You fucking lie down on the bed, now."

"No."

"Do it, or I'll make you."

"No!"

He dragged her to the bed. She kicked and screamed, her ears ringing from her protests. "Let me go. Stop it, Daniel. I mean it!" He pushed her down, and she fought him like a wild thing. "I won't love you anymore if you do this. I won't love you anymore!"

He pinned her with the weight of his body, stealing her breath. He dragged her hands over her head and held them there. *I'm afraid. Don't let me go.* She was terrified he would give up on her and give her the distance she fought for. She chanced a look at him, almost too afraid to see what he thought. *Please understand me. I want this, but I don't want this. I want you, but I'm scared.*

He tightened his hands on her wrists, his gaze never leaving hers.

"You're mine, Wed. I'm sorry you don't like it sometimes. But what's true is true."

She moaned. "Daniel..."

He loved her. There was no other message to glean from his eyes. She pressed against him miserably, and he nuzzled her as she went passive and limp under him. When he let go of her arms, she wrapped them around his neck like a drowning girl. Hot tears fell on her cheeks, tears she hadn't even been aware of.

"Shh, okay. It's okay." He soothed her, dropping intermittent kisses on her lips, her ears, her neck, her tear-streaked cheeks. She could feel her tension and wildness ebbing away as he drew her close. "Okay, Wed, I've got you. Everything's okay now."

"It's not okay," she sobbed.

"It is okay, baby. Look at me."

"No."

"Look at me."

"I don't want to."

"Why not?"

"I...I can't."

"Why can't you?"

"Because...because I don't know. I don't know what's wrong with me."

"Nothing's wrong with you, baby. Nothing's wrong with you, except that you're really afraid of intimacy. Like, phobia afraid." He slowly parted her legs. "But it's okay. We're working on it, aren't we? Yes, that's a good girl."

She shook her head, even as she buried her face in his neck and pulled him closer. The warm, familiar scent of him soothed her racing heartbeat to a plodding ache. *Don't let go of me. Please. Please. Please.*

"That's better," he said. "Don't fight me. It's so much easier if you don't fight me." He traced over her stilled, conquered body, drawing delicious lines of warmth all over. He was casting a net, and she was caught in it. He moved his hand lower to cup her pussy. "Wed, I know exactly what's wrong."

"You don't."

"Yes, I do. You get afraid sometimes that if you let yourself love me, you'll end up hurt again."

"No," she moaned. "No. Maybe."

"That I won't be there when you need me to take care of you. That I won't love you back. I know you really, really want to protect yourself. But don't you get tired of worrying about it all the time?"

She shook her head, shuddering in his arms.

"I'll always take care of you, Wednesday. I love you. Always. Who's in charge of you, baby?"

"You are," she whispered after a long pause.

"Yes, I am. I'm going to fuck you now, because you belong to me, and I love you very much. Put your arms around me and hold on tight, because I'm going to fuck you and remind you that you're mine."

She shivered as he nudged inside her. She was still crying. She cried because he was right about all of it. He knew her, everything about her, for all she tried to hide it.

"Who loves you, Wed?"

Slippery, slow strokes and his whole body covering hers.

"You do. You."

"Yes, I love you."

She still fought him as he fucked her. She could feel the vitality of his dominance in his grunts and sighs, in his straining muscles. He fucked her until she shook from the fervor of connection, until her nails dug into his fingers where he held her hands. Her orgasm was a gradual build that racked her when it came, endless, enveloping joy that wasn't just her pelvis, her clit, her pussy contracting. It was all of Daniel sliding over her and loving her with complete abandon and courage. When she heard him moan and sigh, she squeezed her pussy around his length, wanting to milk him and contain him. She pressed against him while he pounded in her and came hard.

Afterward he pulled her up and over his lap and spanked her. He held her tight, and she gave free rein to her cries and jerks at the painful blows. It wasn't a very long spanking, just a reconnection, a resetting. He sent her to stand facing the wall when he was done. She leaned her forehead against the cool surface, the outline of his hand on her ass cheeks burning like an emotional brand. *I know you really, really want to protect yourself. But don't you get tired of worrying about it all the time?*

Yes, she was tired of worrying, but the alternative—trusting—was such a risk. Vincent had wished her love and inspiration. Pretty words, but a pipe dream. *A soul mate, to know and understand you.* How was that possible? She didn't even understand herself.

Daniel called her back, and she crawled into his lap, still sniffling. She shifted on her sore cheeks, trying to get comfortable. He rubbed her shoulders, holding her close. When he spoke, each word resonated with quiet gravity.

"I'm not trying to own you, Wed. Not in a malicious way. I'm trying to love you, the way I think you like to be loved." He ran a hand down her arm and squeezed her lightly. "You like control. You like to be told what to do."

"Yes, sometimes. I like it sometimes." She pulled away and frowned at him. "But if I move in here with you..."

"What will happen? We might have some fun? We might grow closer, more committed?" He gave her an arch look. "How could I be such a horrible person to ask for some commitment from you?"

"You don't want commitment. You want control. You want to control me all the time."

"Because I want you to move in here, because I want to be close to you, that means I want to control you? *He* controlled you, Wed, not me. I give you so much more than him, so much more than just control."

She pushed away from him and went to stand by the wall, throwing her arms open in frustration. "I'm not with him anymore! How long are you going to hold that crime over my head?"

"What are you talking about?"

"I'm ashamed enough, without you throwing my relationship with Vincent in my face every fucking time."

"Ashamed? What? I don't throw it in your face."

"You just did. You do it constantly, all the time."

"Constantly? What the fuck are you talking about?"

"God, sometimes it feels like the two of you are still sharing me!"

He shook his head, but something in his expression made the hair rise on the back of her neck. He shook his head again, more forcefully.

"I'm not sharing you with anybody, and you know I fucking never will. Maybe that's what's wrong. Maybe you want me to. Maybe I'm just not enough for you."

"Again! See, you did it again. I'll always be Vincent's slut to you. That girl who let him share me with whoever he wanted. You have no respect for me. You never have."

"Wednesday," he warned.

"You hate me for having been with him, for being the way I was then."

He was staring at her, flabbergasted. Really? He didn't understand that? Was it her problem, then? Everything was her fault. It seemed suddenly there was such distance between them, an impossible distance. Miles and miles from where she stood to where he sat on the bed.

"Come here," he said. His face looked tortured. "Please come here."

For a moment she thought of running, turning and leaving his house forever. She felt like she was standing in a doorway from which she could move forward to him, into love and chance and risk, or from which she could run backward and be safe. She wrung her hands for just a second before her feet moved. Moved toward him.

When she came near, he pulled her closer, so she was standing between his legs, against his chest. She laid her head beside his neck, listening to the sound of the blood beating in his veins.

"Do you really believe that?" he asked. "Do you believe I have no respect for you? That I...hate you?"

"Daniel," she whispered. "I just don't think I'll ever be able to give you all you need."

He rested his hand on her neck, squeezing softly. "You listen to me, Wednesday. I love you. I adore you. Just as you are." He hugged her tighter, cupping her ass with his other hand. "As for shame, you will never again utter that word to me. Or think it or feel it, concerning the way I love you. Do you understand me?"

She moved her head and felt a tear drop onto her cheek, then slide down to her chin.

"Do you understand me, Wednesday Carson?"

After a long, quiet moment, she whispered, "I love you."

He kissed her cheeks and her eyelids, the sensitive spot beneath her ear. Each time he kissed her, she said it again. "I love you." The world didn't stop. The sky didn't fall. She threaded her fingers into his hair and pressed her forehead against his. "Are you sure you want me to move in?" she asked. "To live here all the time?"

"Yes."

"Okay."

"Well, look—What?"

"Okay. I'll move in."

He seemed at a loss for words. Apparently he had prepared himself for more argument, not capitulation.

"Well, good," he managed finally. "When?"

"Whenever you want. Sometime next week. But I'll need some concessions."

"What kind of concessions?"

"I want to have some time to myself. Some time when I'm not at your command."

"Okay. You'll have plenty of time on your own. I do work, you know."

"So do I," she said. "When I get home, I won't always feel like dropping to my knees and sucking your cock."

"Okay, fair enough. You'll be allowed whatever time you need off the clock."

"And I want my own room."

"No," he said at once.

"Yes."

"I want you with me. I want you to sleep next to me every night."

"I will sleep with you. But I want my own room to have a place to go, a place for when I need to be alone."

"Fine," he said. "You can have your own room, but you will never lock me out."

"I can't promise that."

"If you lock me out, I get to paddle your bottom."

"Okay."

"And you're in my bed every night. Every night," he said. "Whether you love me or hate me or wish me to hell."

"Every night. I'll be there."

"I won't even put a bed in your room."

"Fine. Maybe you can just put a pan of bread and water on the floor and some hooks on the wall for me to hang from."

"I've been thinking we should experiment with some hooks and chains. I see you've been thinking it too. Maybe I'll buy you another of those old collars you used to wear."

She rolled her eyes. "Why don't you trick my room out like a dungeon? We'll spend today painting the walls black."

"Hmmm. Might be hard to explain when company comes."

"Especially when the rest of your house is so fucking white."

"Possibilities," he said. "Possibilities."

CHAPTER NINE

Daniel sat by the window, watching, a faint smile on his face. Wednesday was in a rush. He had made her late again. She came bounding down the stairs, her curls bouncing, and flashed him a vicious look.

"Be careful, darling. Or I'll make you even later."

He could tell she rolled her eyes, even looking at the back of her head. She grabbed her bag and glanced over at him. He smirked back. *Yes, I'm watching you, Wed. Of course I am.* With a sigh, she grabbed an apple off the counter. Breakfast was a strict household rule. Wednesday hated to eat breakfast, but Daniel insisted on it.

Of all the rules he forced her to follow, most of them perverted sexual rules, the ones that annoyed her most were the simple ones concerning her health. *Eat breakfast. Sleep well. Don't bottle your feelings. Exercise. Laugh every day.* He insisted on these rules because he loved her. He told her so often. Maybe someday she would believe him.

Sweet girl, she was so cute and fuckable in her office clothes. Stylish suit and shiny pumps, and yes, a garter belt and stockings underneath most days. She had plenty of sets to choose from—he must have bought her fifty by now. She said wearing them to work reminded her of him while she was away. Sometimes it was all he could do not to fall on her as she headed out the door, and now was one of those times. She gazed at him from across the kitchen.

"I'm not coming over there."

"I'll be good. I promise."

"You've already made me late."

"I'm sorry," he said. "Come over here. Let me apologize properly."

She fought a smile. "I'm serious. You have to let me go."

"I will. Just one little kiss good-bye."

She walked over to him like she was approaching a wild lion. He was sure what he was feeling was written all over his face—and in the tent of his pants—but he played tame. All he did was lay a passionate kiss on her, one he hoped she'd remember all day.

"I had fun last night," he whispered, caressing her beautiful bottom over her skirt.

"I did too," she said, her eyes shining. Then she pushed away. "I'm going to be so late."

"Do you want me to drive you?"

"No. I'll see you later."

He watched her ass sway as she walked out the door, then slammed it behind her. He fucking hated it when she left.

Of course, he had numerous naughty fantasies of her at work to occupy him throughout the day. Well, when did he *not* have naughty fantasies of Wednesday? But the work ones were some of the more exciting ones, because she had forbidden him to visit her there. She found it too difficult to concentrate when there was a chance he might pop in, so after a couple of breathless, tempting visits, he had agreed it was probably better to leave her to her tasks.

But he still had fantasy visits. Oh yes. He visited her office regularly in his mind. He pictured her leaning over a manuscript, her reading glasses on the end of her nose, her legs crossed under the desk, the tops of her stockings peeking out from beneath her pencil skirt. He would knock on the door, and she'd look up at him and part her lips ever so slightly. He'd come in and lock the door, order her to her knees. Or bend her over the desk, spreading her legs wide with his feet. *I'm going to start in your pussy and finish in your ass*, he'd say with a growl. Papers would scatter, phones would knock off the hook, pens and paper clips would go flying. Her moans would get so loud he'd have to muffle them with his hand.

Ah, he burned for her. That morning she'd been in fine form. Once hadn't been enough, not even close. She'd gotten up to shower for work and waved her backside at him, that curvy ass of hers still crisscrossed with marks from last night. Jesus Christ, what did she think would happen? He'd ordered her to her knees in an instant.

She could have said no. She hadn't had her stockings on at that time, after all. They had struck on an arrangement soon after she agreed to move in with him. She would always be his girlfriend, his love, his charming submissive, but when she had on a garter belt and stockings, she was his slave. He could do to her as he wished, no matter how unreasonable or depraved his needs were. At those times there was no "no," no slow obedience, no smirks or laughter or moods.

At those times there was only him and his base desires, and her body for him to use as he wished.

So far their little stocking system had worked out well for both of them. She liked the clear delineation of the degree of obedience he would expect from her, and for him, there was that delicious thrill when he'd send her to put on the stockings. He obsessed over it, ordering her off to dress in that silk and lace. In quiet moments, he'd rehearse the perfect words to say. He could have sent her running for them at any time with merely a look, but he enjoyed it much more to send her off with some blunt, explicit words.

Go put on some stockings, he might say. *At once.* Short and simple. Always effective.

Or he might say, *Wednesday, I feel like fucking. Fucking every hole you have. Go put on your stockings so I can use you l like a whore.* More creative, and she always thrilled to the expletives.

Or he might say, *Wednesday, stockings, now. Kneel on the bed and wait for me.* And he would make her wait, sometimes for an hour, and get wet for him on her hands and knees.

Or he might say, *Wednesday, put on your stockings, I think you need some discipline. I want to put some marks on your ass.* She would scurry off without a word or hesitation, anxious to take whatever he would give her.

It wasn't long before he began to obsess over stockings. Since meeting Wednesday, he couldn't pass a lingerie store without ducking inside. He sprang huge erections choosing provocative ensembles for his lover. The shopgirls were always discreet, pretending not to notice. Stockings, garters, and corsets haunted his every dream. Lace tops stretched on trembling thighs, straight back seams, beribboned garter clasps. He always, always woke up hard.

After their sessions, as soon as he released her, Wednesday would usually go off to her room. White bed, white linens, white walls, white furniture, white carpet.

Possibilities.

And yes, there was a bed in there, even though he had denied it to her at first. She said she needed a bed to truly relax, which he understood. He had ordered her a luxe one, massive and expensive and, yes, pristine white. He'd had it outfitted with crisp white French sheets and a white satin comforter that had cost a small fortune. It was an offering for his goddess, an altar for her, and they never besmirched it with sex. At least not yet, though he'd often find her dead asleep in that bed after their sessions. Before he went to sleep, he'd go and get her and carry her in his arms back to where she belonged.

She didn't always run off afterward, though. After hard sessions, really hard ones, she would stay with him. Sometimes he would take her to his studio and paint her. Sometimes, instead, he took her to bed. He'd undo her lingerie, the hooks, the laces, the clasps, and lay her down. He would caress her all over, and worship her and love her and fuck her gently until she trembled in his arms and came.

Was it an apology for the rougher pleasures? He knew she thought it was, but no, it wasn't that. It was more like a thank-you. *Thank you, Wednesday, for trusting me to use you. Thank you, Wednesday, for being so vulnerable to me. Thank you, Wednesday, for being brave when I hurt you. Thank you, Wednesday, for letting me lose my mind.*

His intrepid, sex-siren-delicious editor. He could have kept her at home like some treasured concubine, paid for everything she needed, but she wanted to work. Lord knew he wanted to keep her home. But

Wednesday truly loved her work. She didn't only do it for security. He told himself she did, to make himself feel better, but the truth was she fucking loved her job.

Unfortunately, she would need to leave it soon, for a while anyway. He hadn't told her yet. He was putting off that conversation, because he knew it would mean an ugly standoff. She was not going to be happy, but he had accepted a design assignment that would take him to an overseas film set for several months. There was not a chance he would attempt it without her. He hated to force it on her, but it couldn't be helped. It was too much of a trial for him to go so much as a day without her now. A week? No, torture. Months? A flat impossibility.

But God, it was going to be wretched. It was going to be a bigger fight than they'd ever had. What would he end up doing? How far would he go to subdue her? Between them, those lines of allowable force sometimes blurred.

* * *

Daniel decided to talk to her on the weekend, but Saturday began with such wonderful intimacy that he pushed it back to Sunday morning, when they ate their favorite foods and lingered at the table. Pancakes, eggs, fruit, mimosas, while they laughed and flirted together. But not this morning, because she knew. She knew exactly what was coming. She knew about the project he'd been hired for, that it would separate them. She knew what he would ask, had known for weeks. But now here it was.

"Wednesday. Can you take some time off work? A leave of absence?"

"For how long?"

You know how long, he wanted to say. "For three months or so. Maybe four."

"Four months? No. They need me at the office. I'll lose my job."

"You can't telecommute? Work online?"

"A lot of the authors are local. It's a face-to-face press. That's our whole shtick, what sets us apart. So no."

They both kept eating. She stabbed her pancakes around in her syrup while he took a sip of his drink.

"Well, you'll need to quit, then, so you can come with me to Australia."

She was quiet a long time. Then she said, "I don't want to quit."

"I know. But you'll have to. There's no other way."

"Can't I visit you? Spend the weekends now and again?"

"Now and again?" He laughed humorlessly. "Now and again doesn't work for me."

"Daniel—"

"It's too much travel anyway to be flying back and forth. I want you to be with me."

"Yes, I know." She said that—*I know*—very snidely, in a tone she would have been punished for in the bedroom.

"Wed." It was a warning.

She put her fork down and folded her arms on the table. "I don't want to quit my job." Not *I'm not going to* or *I won't* or *No fucking way.* Just *I don't want to,* because she knew she would whether she wanted to or not.

He looked back at her. *It is what it is.* He tried to look sympathetic. He tried.

"I knew you were going to do this." She pushed back from the table and stormed off. He cornered her in the living room by the birch tree. She stood behind it, as if she could hide there from him.

"No shit, Wed. What else can I do? What did you expect? That I could piss off from you for four months? That it would be okay? No fucking chance."

"It's my job, Daniel. It's my livelihood!"

"And you're my submissive! You don't need to work."

"I want to work. I love my work."

"You claim to love me too."

She snorted and threw up her hands. "Oh, either I quit my job or I don't love you. Nice."

"You belong with me. I'm not leaving you here. You can always get another job. The day we get back you can go out and apply somewhere, and they'd hire you in a heartbeat."

"That's not the point. What makes you think you're entitled to this? You think you own me!"

"Yes, we've discussed this before. I do."

"No, you don't." The foot stamp. Classic. "You don't own me."

He cocked his head to the side. "Don't make me show you. Not now, when I'm angry. When you're angry."

"I'm not angry." She made fists at her sides. "I'm bored. I'm tired of you always acting like this. You're so possessive, Daniel, always! *Mine, mine, mine, mine, mine.* How about letting me be my own person and have my own fucking life? Are you that afraid I'll run off? Sometimes you're pathetic. Sometimes it's pathetic how you cling to me. How needy you are."

He was on her before she'd even finished talking. Her careless words—they made him see red. He took her face between both his hands, not gently, and hissed at her.

"You listen to me, you crazy fuck. The only thing I need is you kneeling at my fucking feet. The only thing I'm afraid of is not being able to choose which of your three holes I want to fuck first. The only thing that's pathetic is how you pretend you don't fucking need me. If anyone is pathetic in this fucking relationship it's you, you damaged little slut."

She slapped him hard, tears shining in her eyes. He barely felt it. He couldn't believe the words had actually come from his mouth. *Damaged little slut.* Stupid, angry words spoken in frustration. God knew he hadn't meant them. She turned and ran up to her room and slammed the door. He could hear her throw the lock from downstairs.

He had told her once that locking him out would get her bottom paddled, but he had a feeling at this point she didn't give a fuck. He didn't go up to her. It was too volatile a moment. She probably would have broken the fucking paddle over his head. Better to let her hide away for now.

The fact of the matter was she had already capitulated. She had known long ago she would be coming with him. This was just the bitter process of coming to terms with it. The final, wrenching concession that she really did belong to him, emotionally if not literally. For her he was sure it felt like a final farewell to her independence. It wasn't, but in her addled mind, it was.

He had a drink, early as it was, but he was still pricked from the words she'd spit at him. *Selfish. Boring. Pathetic. Needy.* Very flattering. After all he'd given her, those careless words had raked a nerve. He waited an hour, justifying it in his mind that she needed to be with him, not just because she was his submissive, but for her happiness, for her safety. Hell, it was what she wanted, what she begged for. Control. Ownership. Care. Halfway across the world, he would be too far away to come quickly if she needed him.

Finally he thought he had collected himself enough to talk to her, to get her to see the truth of things. That she had to be with him, that she could return to her job later. That this was necessary. That she needed him too, despite her reckless words.

He trudged up the stairs to her room. He knocked on the door, and she opened it. Her face was drawn and pale. She'd cried hard. He looked down at her, tracing the shadows of the tears on her cheek, then cupped her face.

"We need to talk."

She shook her head, putting her hand over his.

"Daniel," she whispered into his palm, "I want to put on some stockings."

Those seven words began their darkest hour. He took her arm and led her to their room. Once there, she put on some stockings, his favorite set. A sleek black corset and fishnet stockings complemented by brazen plum lipstick. Then she smiled a smile he didn't recognize and gave herself over to him.

And he took her. God, he took that girl. He took her until his fucking nerves started to fray. He took her until he started to feel sick, because she stubbornly gave and took nothing in return. She gave him back nothing, no sighs, no shudders, no bright eyes or small twitches, no resistance, nothing. Nothing at all, but a body to fuck. He fucked her every way he knew how, every way that usually got a reaction. Nothing from her but resigned acquiescence. Her mumbled answers to his ever-more-abhorrent demands were robotic and dull.

She was making her point, and it fucking inflamed him. *I'm here at your feet, Daniel, your three holes to use.* He goaded and tested her, pushed her over the line and further, black temper and fury. She took it in stony silence. *Here's your damaged slut, Daniel. Do your worst.*

He did. He did his very worst to her, hating himself the entire time. It was warfare, and it was ugly. When sex didn't break her, he turned to sadism. He cycled through every angry toy he had, every instrument of torture, to no avail. He couldn't believe they could be so cruel to each other, he to her body and she to his mind. Neither of them flinching, both of them hurting, trapped in this unending scene from hell. She was using the only power she had left, and she was using it to hurt him. It infuriated him. It made him wild. It made him want to jump off a building.

They hadn't used safe words, not since she'd moved in, but she could have blurted them out anytime, and he'd have backed away. They hadn't used them, because they were past that stage. They were so far past it, which was a shame, because they could have used those words now. If she would have said *Untie me, Daniel,* whispered it, screamed it, whatever, they could have let it end. But she didn't, and he kept on and on at her, determined to find her breaking point no matter how long it took.

It took hours and hours. Fucking hours. They went at it for hours, and she never cracked. He never broke her, though he tried it all.

He was the one who gave up in the end.

He yanked her up off the floor, and tore away what was left of the stockings. He crushed the corset in his fists, twisting the boning. Then he balled them all up and threw them in the trash. He never wanted to see them on her again. He had a serious urge to throw it all on a bonfire, every stocking and garter in the house.

"Get out." He pointed at the door. "Fucking get out."

She stormed off, not looking at him, and he slammed the door behind her. He needed to get ahold of himself. He stood with his fists clenched for several minutes, listening to his heart race. He knew he should leave her alone right now, but he couldn't let it end this way. He was the Dominant. It was up to him to set things back to rights when they went sideways and all to hell.

After a few more quiet moments, he felt calm enough. He yanked the door open and strode down the hall to her room. Her door was open, and he saw the red splotches all over her white comforter before anything else. His heart seized, but then he saw her over by the wall, and the smell registered.

Paint. The rest of the canister was turned over on the carpet, carelessly, on purpose. He stood and stared, but if she knew he was there, she was ignoring him. She had a can of red paint in one hand and a brush in the other. She had painted words in huge, broad strokes across two whole walls: YOU DON'T OWN ME.

And under that, even larger, in big red letters, she was finishing the words YOU NEVER WILL.

She threw the can down when she was done, and turned to him, ferocious, livid. She wasn't Wednesday. She was some monster he'd created, some cauldron of fury and hate. She leaned down in a graceful, fluid movement and ran her hands across the river of bloodiness on the carpet. She slapped it on the wall over and across the painted words, red punches and handprints. She came at him then and pushed him, marking him too. She made a sound like a scream, only more feral, then spun away, pulling clothes on over the paint. He stared dumbly at his angry marks on her body—every bit as starkly visible as her words on the wall.

"Jesus, Wed," he finally said helplessly.

But by then she was already gone.

* * *

Wednesday dreamed of red paint and black stockings. She dreamed of his face, angry and cruel, then shocked. Defeated, at the end. She lay on her friend's futon in the new clothes she'd had to buy, and counted the days, wishing for him to call but knowing he wouldn't. She wondered if he would think she had gone to Vincent. Let him think so. Let him hurt the way she did. She hated him. Still, she cried for him every night.

Red and black colored all her memories. She couldn't get a clear view in hindsight of what had gone wrong and how they'd both gotten so angry. Because he'd asked her to quit her job?

But he hadn't asked; he had demanded. If he'd just asked her, she would have said yes. She had written all over his walls. *You don't own me. You never will.* She had destroyed his pristine white room in his pristine white house. The pristine room he kept for her so she would feel treasured and comfortable. She had defaced the white satin comforter that had made her gasp in delight the first time she saw it, thinking it the most beautiful one on earth. She'd wrapped it around herself and thought how much he must love her. Then she'd splashed paint all over it, destroyed it and the carpet too.

No more possibilities. It had felt like bloodletting. Had she lost her mind? She thought they both must have, and she wanted to tell him she was sorry, but she'd hoped he would say he was sorry first. She could forgive him if he apologized. She would quit her job and follow him to Australia. She'd follow him anywhere, because that was how much she loved him. He didn't know where she was, but he could at least call her cell...

A week went by, and she stopped waiting. She told herself it was better if they never spoke again. She decided to send some work friends over to get her stuff from Daniel's, but somehow she never remembered to ask them. She certainly couldn't face him herself after what she'd done to his house with his red paint and brushes. That house was always too damn bright and perfect. He was too bright and perfect, with his intimacy and healthy relationships. When he'd decided he wanted her, he'd made a huge mistake. He certainly realized that now. It was for the best.

But she looked at her calendar every night and thought about Daniel flying to Australia. He would be so, so far away. Soon his trip was only a week away. Six days, five days until he left. She craved him like air and water. Soon he would be gone! She knew when he left, it would mean forever.

Her mind tried to move past him, but her heart was wild with grief. *Call him. Just call him.* She handled her phone, opening and closing it, imagining her fingers pushing the numbers. She tossed and turned at night, thinking of what to say to him. She remembered his anger when she'd defied him, when she'd refused to react to him. She remembered the defeated look on his face when he'd stared into that room and seen she'd gone crazy. Whenever she closed her eyes at night, big black letters danced behind her lids.

Four days. Three days. Only three days! That night, while rain beat against the window, she cried until she could barely breathe. *Call me, Daniel. Why won't you call?* Then she realized why he hadn't called. He still probably thought she wouldn't go. What else would he think after the way she'd acted?

He thought she wouldn't, but she would.

She took a cab to his house and stood outside, too afraid to knock on the door. What if he didn't want her anymore? What if he wasn't even there? What if he'd left for Australia three days early? She dug for her phone. Her fingers shook as she called his number. There was no time anymore to figure out what to say. He answered before the phone had even finished ringing once.

"Wednesday, honey—"

"Daniel!" Her words spilled out in desperation. "Daniel, please let me come back. I'll pay for everything I ruined. I'm sorry. I'll fix your room back the way you had it. I'll make it all white again." There was a long pause, and she thought maybe he'd hung up. "Daniel? Are you there?"

"I'm here, Wed. Jesus. Honey, it was your room." He sounded kind, not angry. "It was your room to destroy. And God, I'm sorry I made you want to do that."

She was quiet, listening to his soft breathing, her heart aching more than ever now that she heard his voice, so familiar and caring, in her ear.

"I want you to come back," he said. "I know you probably don't want to, and I definitely don't deserve you, but I want you to come back to me. You can keep your job. We'll figure out how to deal with being apart. I just got so caught up in the D/s shit and the ownership thing. I went totally over the line. I'm so sorry, Wed, but...baby girl...I'm leaving Monday."

"I know," she said. "I want to come."

"You do?"

"Yes, I want to come with you. Can I? If you still want me to come."

"Of course I do. Where are you? Where are you right now?"

"I'm outside. I just got out of a cab."

"You're outside where? Outside my house?"

"It's raining out here, and it's cold," she said. "Can I come in?"

* * *

Miracle of miracles. Wednesday. He'd been so sure she was gone forever. All the happiness she'd brought him, her smiles, her myriad moods and expressions all gone away. He'd barely functioned since he'd driven her off. Sometimes he punished himself by imagining she'd fled back to Vincent. He would shake with anxiety picturing her cowering under his hand, kneeling at his feet beside Samantha.

But no, she was here at his door with red-rimmed eyes, her arms wrapped around herself. Then she was inside his house, in his foyer, dripping wet, cold rain on his floor. He closed the door, and for a minute he just touched her hair, the damp curls cold and soft under his hands.

"You're all wet." He went to grab a towel and tried to think of what to do, what to tell her. He had to say exactly the right thing so she'd never go away again. "Wed..." His voice sounded strained, but then she launched herself into his arms, and after that there was no need to say anything.

He took her straight to bed and held her while she cried, cried too hard to tell him where she'd gone, how she'd been. He held her close, and they talked in whispers. They didn't say much, just heartfelt *I'm sorrys* and *why?s* and pleas for forgiveness. He insisted it was all his fault. He was the Dominant—he should have had better control. But she shook her head and said she had stolen his control on purpose.

"Why did we hurt each other?" she whispered, so tired her eyes were closing. "Let's never, ever do it again."

In the morning, he reached for her tentatively, unsure of his reception. She turned to him without hesitation and took his cock in her hands. She would have ducked under the covers and started to suck him, but he stopped her. He wanted her near, not down between his legs. He pulled her under him and aligned her warm, lithe body to his. Her hips to his hips, her thighs to his thighs, her heart to his heart, and his lips against her neck, licking her pulse. He wrapped his hands in her hair and kissed her, an endless kiss. Somewhere in the middle of it, he parted her legs and entered her. He hugged her so close while he fucked her that he could feel every breath, every flex of muscle, every heartbeat. *Wednesday.*

They lay still a long time afterward, until his perpetually hard cock finally grew soft and slipped from her. He made her stay and rest while he brought breakfast, and they fed each other in bed. While they ate, he spoke of his efforts to repair her room, shushing her continued apologies and offers to pay for the damage.

He told her she could choose a new room if she wanted, and make it different if the memories would be bad. She didn't answer. She just got up and padded down the hallway. He followed and stood outside the door, watching her. She looked at the room a long time. It really did look nearly the same as before. New carpet, new white satin comforter. Many coats of white paint on the walls until those words were obliterated. While she looked, he gazed at her back and remembered that awful Sunday when her ass had been so red and bruised from their standoff. He marveled at how white and unmarked her skin was now, completely pristine, as it hadn't been since she moved in.

She reached to smooth the comforter on the bed.

"How many coats did it take?"

"A few," he said. She laughed softly, and he did too.

"Thank you for fixing it back the way it was."

"It was all I could do. I didn't feel like I could come after you, so I did this instead."

"Why did you feel you couldn't come for me?"

He sighed. "Because I didn't feel I deserved you back. I still don't. Where were you, by the way?"

"A friend's," she said after a moment. She didn't go into specifics, but he knew she hadn't been with Vincent, or she would have been marked.

"I would have come for you eventually. After I got back from Australia. When I was nearly mad."

She looked doubtful. "You'd have found someone else by then."

"Do you think so? It took years and years for me to find you."

"You would have found some lovely submissive somewhere."

"More lovely than you? I don't think one exists."

Of course he meant it from the bottom of his heart, but she gave him that doubtful smile that always made him want to shake her. *Jesus*, he thought. *Why don't you look in the mirror?*

She did look in the mirror then, but she was looking back at him. Without meaning to, he glanced over at the wall. The words were still there, for both of them. No doubt they always would be. But she was there in his house with the intention to stay, and he bought luggage and travel things for her the next day. She settled matters at work and said good-bye to her friends. When she finally started packing, he worked alongside her, offering advice of what to take, what traveled well. So he knew when she went to the armoire and rustled through it, choosing some sets of corsets, garters, and stockings to carefully pack alongside the other things.

And since Wednesday packed the costumes, he thought it only right that he pack the props. He collected all his favorite instruments of torture and tucked them into her bag. She made no comment, only continued to pack as usual. He sincerely hoped no one demanded to inspect her luggage.

After they packed, they fucked, fast and rough. They did it right on the floor, because her suitcases were still on the bed. It was a welcome back and an *I've missed this* fuck. It was a fuck to say to her, *You won't be sorry. I promise to be better from now on.*

10 CHAPTER TEN

The night before they left, he decided to take her out to dinner at the same fancy restaurant he'd taken her on their first date.

"And Wednesday," he said as she left to get ready, "I'd like you to wear stockings under your dress."

"Yes, Daniel."

She said it like a perfect little slave, and he stared at her across the table for two hours like she was one. She shifted under his gaze all through dinner while he stared silent promises at her. That was why he'd taken her there, because it took so long to eat. He loved to anticipate the pleasure of fucking her. He loved to watch her squirm, his submissive impatient and hot with lust. He loved watching her and knowing she was his to use at his leisure.

All the way home, she fidgeted in the car until he scolded her to stop. She pressed her legs together and looked out the window.

"Yes, Daniel," she said in that way that made him wild.

Back home, they didn't make it past the foyer. He bent her over the table right there and unfastened his pants. He'd had every intention of making her suck him, but he found he had to be inside her that very second. She moaned as he entered her, and her hands searched frantically for purchase. He knew she needed to be restrained at times like these. He trapped her hands in his and held them hard at the small of her back. They both came less than a minute later, nearly knocking over the table. She laughed as he bit the back of her neck and then licked away the sting. He unzipped her dress and pulled it over her head, running his hands over her breasts and the flare of her hips.

"Upstairs," he said. "Playtime's over."

In the bedroom, she turned and faced him. God, she was beautiful, so beautiful and brave in her midnight blue garter belt and stockings. He tore out of his clothes and sat on the bed, patting his lap. She knew what to do, draping herself across his broad thighs. He didn't spank her right away. He spent some time just looking her over, and she waited, not squirming or tensing. He had taught her that, to relax across his lap and wait. Then he gathered her hands in his and held them tight. He spanked her for a long time, longer than he had thus far in their relationship.

He started out softly, just making her bottom flush pink. He got gradually harder, so the pain was always there for her, but he didn't really mark her, didn't really bruise her until nearly the end. She was crying by then, sobbing into his leg, gorgeous whimpers and pleas. He loved the sounds she made, and he paused to reach down and caress her lips. She nibbled and licked at his fingers. He knew he would have to let her come soon.

He was hard again by that time, so he tumbled her onto the bed and arranged her on her hands and knees. He reached around for her soaking clit. Jesus, she loved to be spanked. He thrust lube deep inside her ass, positioned the head of his cock at her hole, and pushed inside. Slowly at first, just the head of his cock, and then, when he felt her relax for him, he took her hard, all the way in. She was so warm and tight, a shivering, shuddering receptacle for his pleasure. She started to cry, not because he hurt her. She cried because she wanted to come, and she knew she wasn't allowed yet.

"Hush. Let me fuck your ass, Wed."

"Please."

"No. It's time you learned patience. Wait for me." He struggled to imbue his voice with some semblance of strictness as he reeled from the sensation of her ass gripping his cock. "Wait for me, or I'll punish you. You know the rules."

She sobbed and shook her head. "I can't, Daniel. I can't!"

And she couldn't. She came a few seconds later. As he'd known she would.

"Naughty," he whispered in her ear. Well, he would punish her later. For the moment he kept fucking her ass, and even though she'd been naughty, he let her come again before he climaxed inside her. He pulled her hair hard as she orgasmed. The feel of her coming and clenching around him always made him insane. He held her close while they struggled for breath together. When he finally drew away from her, she collapsed on the bed.

"Oh no," he said. "We're not finished yet for the night. You came without permission."

"I know, Daniel." She looked too fuck-happy to care.

All their toys were packed, the clamps and whips and restraints. He improvised and returned to the old standard, his thick leather belt. That lovely little pervert—just the sound of him pulling it from his pants had her grinding against the bed.

"Don't you dare." He doubled the belt over and pulled her hands up roughly to grasp the iron bed frame. "You hold on here, and you don't let go, girl. And don't even think of coming. You're being punished."

"Yes, Sir." She was still grinding against the bed, just more furtively. He gave her a sharp crack on her bottom.

"I mean it."

He gave her twenty, which was the agreed-upon penalty for coming without his permission, but it was a losing battle when she was in this mood. She did come again, sobbing with satisfaction and release, so he added twenty more, because to let it go would have disappointed them both. Afterward he lay awake and looked at her as she slept, at her marked bottom and thighs, at the lacy stockings that haunted his dreams.

Just a few hours later they were holding hands on a plane to Australia. Every so often, she shifted uncomfortably on the soft first-class seat. Then their eyes would meet and they'd smile at the secret they shared.

He had her again, and she had him. God, she had him.

* * *

Ah, Wednesday mused. Airplane daydreams. Or night dreams, rather. Something about the persistent hum and claustrophobic closeness of an airplane cabin lent itself to wanderings of the mind.

It was late at night, and the cabin was dark. Daniel was awake, concentrating on his set-design plans, but she was night dreaming, and her panties were getting more soaked by the minute. They'd been traveling all day, it seemed. Who knew it took so long to reach the Australian outback? But she wasn't doing so badly, preoccupied by the delicious memories of their playtime the night before. God, he had fucked her and spanked her and fucked her and spanked her some more. He was the most virile and energetic lover she'd ever known, and the most talented too. More than that, he was a kind, loving man. She didn't know why she'd pushed him away for so long. She belonged with him always, right next to him.

She shifted in her seat, pressing her thighs together. She could still remember the feel of his cock in her, hard and thick. She wished they weren't on a plane, even a darkened plane with their own aisle in first class. She wished they weren't on a plane, because she really wanted to attack him right then. It was all she could do not to sigh in frustration as she squirmed beside him, grinding subtly against the wide, comfortable seat.

"Little Miss Wednesday," Daniel murmured, not even glancing up from his laptop. "What are you doing over there?"

She blushed hot. Caught. The man somehow noticed every minute shift of her body, every flex of muscle. She looked over at him, at his brows drawn together as he studied his laptop screen. She could see, though, the tiniest hint of a smile at the corner of his lips.

"I'm just thinking," she said with as much innocence as she could muster.

He laughed. "Thinking about what?"

Oh, as if he didn't know. She shifted again and gave him a look. He looked back at her, then started closing his program. "Go to the bathroom and take off your panties, then come back here. Go. Now."

"Right now?" She looked around at the other passengers to see if anyone had overheard his quiet words. To her relief, it seemed most of them were sleeping.

"If I have to ask twice, you'll be sorry later. I won't spank you on the airplane, but we'll be going straight to the hotel when we arrive, and we'll have a very private and soundproof room."

Point taken. He moved his legs to let her get by, not missing the opportunity to stick his hand up her skirt. His fingers grazed the tops of her thigh-high stockings. No garters on this trip. It was way too long.

"Hurry." His whispered order had her knees going weak. She couldn't meet his eyes. She walked down the aisle feeling already naked. His piercing eyes and insistent demands had a way of doing that to her.

She wedged herself into the tiny airline bathroom and looked for a moment in the mirror. In the harsh light she looked pale. Her eyes were wide, her pupils dilated, as if reflecting the primitive effect he had on her. She reached under her skirt to pull off her panties, and just as she suspected, they were soaked through. She knew he would take them from her when she returned to her seat and inspect them himself and whisper to her, *naughty...*

Crap. She hadn't even brought her bag with her. Her skirt had no pockets, nor did her top, so she balled the silk panties up in her fist and took a deep breath before opening the door. If she had felt naked on the way to the bathroom, she felt ten times more naked on the way back. Daniel watched her return, his eyes alive with that light she had come to recognize well. His lips held back a smile, but she saw it dancing around the edges.

Again, he shifted to let her move past him. "Give me," he said before she'd even taken her seat.

"Daniel!" she pleaded softly, looking around the cabin.

"Give them to me."

She handed them over, damp and crumpled, and flushed while he manipulated the small scrap of silk in his broad palm.

"Now, Wednesday." He leaned toward her with a wicked smile. "You are going to sit still there in that seat, and you're going to tell me exactly what you were thinking to make these panties so wet. You're going to use lots of descriptive details, and you're not going to fidget like that."

She tried hard to still the unconscious and desperate press of her legs against the seat. Her clit was throbbing at this point. Oh yes, he was planning to play with her, and he was going to play with her for a while. Well, it was a long flight for him too, so she couldn't really blame him. She thought for a moment, planning her words, then she leaned close to him.

"I was thinking about last night. About the things you did to me."

"What things? Specifics."

"I was thinking about the look you gave me before you pulled me over your lap. The way you looked at me, it made me want to do anything for you." She breathed the word *anything*, infusing it with all the love and lust she felt. He shifted beside her.

"Then, when you pulled me over your lap, I remember the feel of your rock-hard thighs, and the feel of your leg hairs tickling me. I wanted to rub my clit against your thighs."

"You did, you silly slut, don't you remember?" She felt his smile against her ear.

"Yes, I did. At least I tried, but you wouldn't let me be bad. Only a little bit bad."

"Yes, you tried hard to be good. I remember, little girl."

"But it was easier when you held my arm to keep me still while you spanked me. I love when you take me in hand like that."

His only answer was to lick her ear.

"After that, remember what you did to me?" she continued in a soft voice. "I can't think of it without getting all wet and crazy for you."

Daniel's face looked hard. "Open your legs." He pulled a blanket over them while she obediently parted her thighs.

God, she was so fucking wet. When he found her clit with his fingers, she couldn't stifle a moan.

"Hush, Wed," he said through gritted teeth. "Don't make a sound. Open my pants and put your hand on my cock."

She did, but she was finding it hard to breathe suddenly.

"Go on," he said as she stroked his rigid length. "Tell me. Tell me why you liked what came next."

"I liked how you pushed me onto the bed and pulled up my hips and made me...made me take you in my ass." She closed her eyes. His fingers were killing her, tormenting her. She could barely put two words together. "I love how it feels when you put the head of your cock against my ass, because I know..." Jesus Christ, she was about to go off. His cock was hard and pulsing while she fondled it.

"Because you know...?" he prompted.

"Because I know how good it's going to feel when you slide all the way into me and fuck me deep. God, Daniel, it feels..." She pressed her forehead against his, gasping for breath. "Daniel!"

"How does it feel?"

"It feels so naughty and intense, and..."

She arched against his hand. He slid two fingers into her, never stopping the maddening teasing of her clit.

"And what?" he asked.

"It feels like I totally belong to you, and I never want you to stop fucking me, ever." She clutched his cock as she came breathlessly, the last of her words a weak exhalation. She tried hard as hell not to moan out loud as his fingers worked her pussy and her walls contracted on them again and again. He didn't take them out of her until she was exhausted and still beside him.

"Daniel," she whispered. She gripped his cock.

"Suck me, Wed. Fucking suck me. Now."

She dived under the blanket. At that point she didn't care if anyone saw, although in the quiet, dark cabin she doubted anyone did, because it took less than a minute for him to finish. She swallowed his hot cum, careful not to spill one drop.

Sheepishly, she emerged from under the blanket, and Daniel smiled at her. "No one saw." He smoothed her mussed-up curls back to rights, then kissed her, deep and hard, his lips overtaking hers.

Finally, limp and satisfied, she sat back in her seat and looked over at him.

"You make me do naughty, naughty things."

He opened his hand, where her now very rumpled and damp panties were still clutched. "I do? I think you're quite naughty without my help."

She snatched them back with a mortified blush.

"Now," he said, "go and put them back on, you naughty, naughty little slut."

* * *

She slept after that, replete with contentment, slept against Daniel's comforting frame while he kept her hand trapped in his. He gently shook her when they were almost to their destination, and kissed her to wakefulness.

"We're almost there, baby."

She stirred, blinking, to find herself staring into his cerulean blue eyes.

"I'm glad you were with me," he said next to her ear. "What a flight."

"Yeah, I agree. I've never been on one quite like it."

"So, are you a new member of the mile-high club?"

"Daniel, I've never even flown first class before, much less sucked someone off under a blanket and had them finger-fuck me until I came."

He laughed, and they stood to gather their belongings. Thankfully their raunchy conversation was drowned out by the bustle of passengers preparing to disembark. She looked around at their tired, blasé faces. They had no idea what she and Daniel had been up to in the wee hours of the morning, she was sure.

They quickly made their way from the airport to the hotel and checked into their room. Daniel teased her again that it was soundproof, but it looked like a regular hotel suite. She wasn't much of a screamer anyway, more the crying and pleading type. Anyway, who would call hotel security and make a report that someone was being spanked?

It was actually a beautiful room, tastefully furnished and decorated with a sitting room and a well-stocked kitchenette. The bathroom was the size of her old apartment, and they had a lot of fun playing around in the two-person shower, helping each other wash off that grimy travel feeling as soon as they arrived. Even so, it was still, essentially, a cold hotel room, and she was relieved that she'd decided to come, for Daniel's sake. She hated to think of him alone on that long flight, then going to sleep in the massive hotel bed all by himself.

Thinking of Daniel and the huge bed together made her clit start to ache again. God, what was wrong with her? Shouldn't she be jet-lagged? She was wide awake, and she wanted to fuck.

She wasn't the only one. Daniel had barely dried off from their shower when he turned to her and fixed her with a look.

"What?" she asked, hugging herself.

A broad, slow smile spread across his face.

"You came on an airplane for the first time last night. Have you ever come in Australia, Wed?"

"I've never even been to Australia. But I'd love to orgasm here, if you think you could arrange that."

"I think I might actually be able to," he said, approaching her like some wild thing stalking its prey.

She started full-on giggling before he even got to her. He looked so horny and fierce. He grabbed her and threw her in the middle of the bed and climbed on top of her while she laughed the whole time. She jumped when he touched her, which made him start laughing and made her laugh harder still. He started to tickle her, the absolute tyrant.

"Shh, shh!" He tried to muffle her with his hand when she started screeching. "This room is not really soundproof."

She could barely catch her breath to laugh at that. She pushed at his hands, begging for respite. "Stop! God, stop. Don't tickle me. Please."

No one on earth was more ticklish than her, and he'd made it his business to learn all her most ticklish spots by heart. She lay under him, gasping for breath, screaming even past the barrier of his hand. He stopped and smiled, tormenting her by wiggling his fingers just above the surface of her skin.

"If I really want to punish you, Wednesday, I should tickle you rather than spank you. I think you hate it worse."

"I do," she said. "Please. Mercy. I'll be good."

He nuzzled her, his fingers finally growing still. "You haven't even been bad, have you? You've actually been very good. I have no excuse to punish you now. That's no fun."

"Maybe you can punish me for not giving you a good reason to punish me."

"You're a genius." He schooled his face to a stern look of reproof. "You naughty girl. How dare you behave when you know I want you to be bad?"

"I'm sorry," she whispered in mock remorse. "I have no excuse for my behavior."

"Hmm," he said with a dramatic sigh. "I suppose you need to be disciplined. You've gotten completely out of hand."

"Spank me. It's the only way I'll ever learn."

His mouth twitched a little at the corner. "Wed, darling, who's in charge here?"

"You are."

"I am, aren't I?"

She nodded, because she didn't trust herself to speak. He arched over her, his hands on either side of her head, and she wanted him to nestle his cock between her legs. He didn't, though, just gazed down at her thoughtfully, brushing the hair back from her eyes.

"Monday."

She giggled. "My name isn't Monday."

"I like to call you Monday sometimes."

She shivered as he licked her neck. "I know. But that's not my name."

He stroked her arm, soft and slow. "Tuesday."

She smothered more laughter. "Daniel, quit."

He traced her jaw, cupped her chin, licking and nibbling her lips. "Thursday."

"Daniel..."

"Friday."

"Please. I asked you nicely to quit."

"Saturday. Sunday. Christmas. Easter. St. Patrick's Day."

"It's Wednesday. You have to face facts."

"Hmm," he said. "I'm partial to Monday."

She rolled her eyes.

"Wednesday," he said softly.

"Yes?"

"I don't feel like spanking you tonight. I'm too tired and too happy to have you here."

"Oh."

"But you know," he continued a moment later, tracing his fingertips lazily up her arm, "I can think of some other ways to torment you. Some very effective and torturous ways."

"Torturous?"

"Mm-hm." He breathed against her neck. "To you, yes." He kissed her, making her shudder, and drew his fingers up the side of her leg. "Put your hands over your head and leave them there."

She did as she was told, and he left her to open her suitcase and root around. He returned with the beautiful white restraints, and heat and pleasure flooded her veins. He knelt beside her and cuffed her hands together with one, then used the other to secure them to the bed. He improvised, since this bed didn't have all the points of attachment their bed did. When he was satisfied she couldn't get away, he leaned back and studied her. His cock was already hard and swollen. She wanted it inside her like nothing else on earth.

He seemed to have other plans for her, though. "Open your legs." She did, but he wasn't satisfied, because he pushed them even wider. He slowly parted her with his hand, drawing the moisture from between her legs up over her clit. He started to caress it—very lightly—and she moaned, arching into his touch. He did it until she started to drift, until the vibrating, building sensation made it hard to lie still. He did it until her breathing grew frantic and labored and her hips were twitching to find that blessed release—

Then he stopped.

She moaned. Oh God. Oh God no. He'd really meant what he'd said about torment. She lay there, frustrated and unsatisfied, while he watched her with a faint smile. Then he said, "Do you want me to taste you? Do you want me to put my mouth on you?"

"Yes. God yes, please, Daniel." She was so hot, so hot from his touch and from the bonds. He knelt between her legs and opened them wide with his shoulders, then lowered his mouth to her mons.

Oh good God, his lips were incredible. His tongue, his teeth—they all worked in perfect harmony, licking and tickling her, conspiring to make her go completely wild. As she writhed and bucked beneath him, there was only one thought in her mind. *Don't stop. Don't stop. Please don't stop until I come.*

But just before she came, the man fucking stopped.

She actually sobbed then. "Daniel, no. Please! Please don't do this to me. You'll kill me."

"Kill you? 'Here lies Wednesday, total drama queen.' I'll visit every week and leave butt plugs on your grave."

She pulled hard at the restraints, but of course there was absolutely nothing to be done. He wouldn't even let her squeeze her legs together. When she tried, he snapped, "Open them!"

He lowered his mouth to one of her nipples. Her scent was on his lips and his tongue. He nibbled and teased her breasts until she cried like a frantic child. He was truly, literally driving her crazy. If he didn't touch her clit, she was going to die. She felt like every ounce of blood in her body was now pooled between her legs, waiting to explode.

"Daniel, this is too mean. You're being too mean to me!"

"Mean? I think I'm being pretty nice. You can't tell me this hurts. You seem to be enjoying it very much, judging from how wet you are." He slid his fingers deep inside her, and she came up off the bed, moaning and panting in desperation. "Yes, definitely wet."

He dived down between her legs again, as soon as she wasn't close enough to come. And, being Daniel, he knew exactly when she was about to come, and at that exact point he left her again. She thought she might have cursed at him then. She couldn't remember. Her brain was too wrecked. He frowned. "Language, Wednesday. You sound like a sailor."

She sobbed. She begged with her gaze. He stroked her hair while she stared and longed for his hard cock. So close, yet so far. He watched her knowingly.

"What do you want, girl? What do you need?"

"Please, please fuck me, Daniel. Please let me come."

He considered. "I'm not sure I've tortured you enough."

"I think you have." She arched her hips toward him. Again, he teased her clit with his fingers. "Don't. Please don't...not unless you'll let me..."

"Let you what?"

"Find some release. I'm dying. You're driving me crazy. Totally crazy!"

"You drive me crazy all the time."

He was merciless. She looked in his eyes, the way he really loved for her to do. She looked deep in his eyes and begged him from her heart. "Daniel, please."

He crawled over her, spreading her wide. She thought she would die from the anticipation of feeling him slide deep inside. But of course, he didn't. She pulled and tore at the restraints in earnest.

"Stop it, baby. You'll hurt your hands." The head of his cock nudged just at the edge of her opening. He slid in a little, then out, a ruthless tease that made her even more frustrated. She closed her eyes and pouted, trying to pretend he wasn't there.

No. He wasn't having that.

"Look at me, Wednesday. Open your eyes."

She did, and whispered, "Please, let me come."

"I want to fuck you first."

"Okay. Yes, fuck me now!"

"Right now?"

If her hands hadn't been restrained, she would have attacked him. "Yes, right now. Please! Right now!"

"You're awfully bossy for a submissive. I think a bossy submissive like you should be put to bed with no orgasm and no cock. Maybe with a toy in your ass and explicit instructions not to touch yourself."

That idea filled her with horror. "I'm sorry. I'm not bossy. I'm desperate."

"Desperately horny," Daniel said.

"Please. Please give it to me!"

"Beg me."

"Please, please give me your fucking cock. Your fat, hard, beautiful cock—please let me have it, Daniel. If you'll just please fuck me now, Daniel, I'm yours, whatever you want!"

"More," he said, and she moaned in frustration.

"Please slide your big, fat cock inside my cunt, please. I'm so wet and hot and horny for you. I'm so fucking wet I'm going to come the second you're in me. Please, give me your cock right now."

"Oh, Wed, I love you so much. If you want me to fuck you, darling girl, then I'll fuck you, and you can come as much as you want."

He slid inside her, a controlled, slow tease. Her walls parted; each inch he entered was an excruciating build to writhing ecstasy. As soon as he filled her all the way, as soon as his hips rested against the insides of her thighs, the last scrap of her control fled. At last she reached that peak and slid down it into pure, mindless euphoria. "Oh, ohhhhhh..." She contracted on his cock, rode it, and let the waves of orgasm combust her. Her pussy felt wrung-out, and her body went completely limp. She closed her eyes, finally satisfied.

He laughed against her lips and whispered, "I'm guessing twice more at least."

She shook her head. She was so spent and so blown away from that massive climax that she couldn't possibly come again. But yes, he did make her come twice more, holding her down, fucking her, devouring her before he came himself with a low groan.

Afterward he lay back beside her, just studying her. He caressed her wrists, which were still tethered to the bed.

"You like this?" she asked. "Seeing me bound up here for you?"

"You know I do." He stroked her shoulder, then down between her breasts to the curve of her hip.

"Why? Why do you like it so much?"

"I guess because it shows how much you trust me."

"How much I trust you?" She laughed. "Quitting my job and flying to Australia with you and a suitcase full of scary toys shows how much I trust you."

"You love those scary toys, Wednesday. You can't live without them. You won't live without them," he added. "I'm sure my itch to spank you will return all too soon. In fact..."

"Oh no."

"While you're already all tied up there..."

She screeched and laughed as he brought his broad hand down on her ass with a stinging slap. Soundproof room or not, that night the other hotel guests got an earful of someone getting spanked, wailing and giggling at the same time.

11 CHAPTER ELEVEN

Wednesday, Wednesday, Wednesday, Wednesday.

That mantra had gotten him through the afternoon's stress and aggravation. He'd already called her from the set to tell her to put on her stockings. What a day.

The project was coming along pretty well, minimal artistic differences and less tantrums by the talent every day, but yeah, there were still tantrums. He was used to them. He worked with these big movie stars all the time. They were a lot like children—pleasant if they got their way, but if you told them no, well...

But he could tell Wednesday no, and she'd bow her head and obey. He could tell Wednesday anything while she had stockings on, and he'd get his way. There was no feeling quite like it, and he loved her for giving that pleasure to him. He stalked through the hotel lobby, his breath tight, his hands in fists. What would she have on up there? Black, white, pink, dark green, lilac, red? He didn't care, as long as there were stockings, as long as she was ready to be under his command for the evening.

He got in the elevator and waited through the climb to their floor. He was already halfway hard just thinking about her. He moved his laptop bag in front of his crotch to hide the growing tent. He breathed a sigh of relief when the elderly couple beside him got off on the fourteenth floor. Only six more floors to the twentieth. *Come on, come on, come on, come on.*

He fumbled with the key, opened the door, and God, there she was.

White. Of course. White was exactly what he needed when he was stressed out like this. She was so elegant, so beautiful. The high garter belt she wore emphasized the curve of her hips, tapering to thin, impossibly graceful legs. Her bra, sheer and corsetlike, pushed up her round, soft breasts like offerings. Clamps—he needed clamps to put on her nipples, and where the hell would he fuck her first?

He crossed the room, shedding his clothes.

"On your knees."

She was down in an instant, her mouth open to receive him. She knew he liked to guide himself to her lips, that he loved to hold her neck and thrust inside, so she waited passively and accepted him almost reverently when he entered her mouth. That gratefulness for cock, that blind desire to please her owner, it was something vanilla women didn't understand.

He pulled her up, and she gave a quick gasp before he kissed her, rough, passionate, deep. He was only getting started for the evening. No one knew that better than she.

"Go kneel on the bed, Wednesday. I want to look at you."

"Yes, Sir." She knelt on the bed, facing away from him, then bent forward from the waist so that her back was arched, her legs spread, her pert bottom cheeks opened just so. He had taught her this, the exact posture he liked. She still had some light marks from the night before, when she'd had a paddling before bed. He looked at her for a while, stroking his half-erect cock, gazing at the ass he'd enjoy later.

He chose a toy to put in her, a small one, because when he finally took her, he wanted it to hurt a little bit. He spread her ass cheeks and inserted the lubed plug carefully. Her flinches and moans were lovely, and his cock twitched again. When the toy was seated and Wednesday was blushing, he ordered her back to her feet.

He went to the drawer in the bedside table to pick out some clamps. They had several pairs, each producing varying degrees of pain. The set he selected wasn't as rigorous as some of the others, so she was able to wear them for a longer time.

He pulled the shelf of her demi-bra down enough on each side to expose her pink nipples. She was so hot already, he barely had to roll them between his fingers before they were as hard as stones. She gazed at him as he attached one clip, then the other. She gasped, fidgeting against the pain, but not protesting. No, never protesting. He met her gaze, and the look she gave him said, *I want to come right now, Daniel, but I'll do as you say.*

There was a delicate chain attaching the silver clips between her breasts, and another longer chain that trailed between her legs. Sometimes he used that longer chain to tether her to something or lead her around, but tonight he attached the clip on the end of it to her clit.

"Walk around," he ordered. She did, without hesitation or protest. She looked beautiful with her features strained and all her most sexual places stinging under his control. The chains swung gently as she moved across the room and back in his direction.

"Touch yourself," he said quietly.

She sucked in a breath and swallowed hard. "Daniel—"

"No, you may not come."

She sighed and reached between her legs with trembling fingers.

"Stroke yourself," he said. "Don't just play around."

"I'll come," she whimpered.

"Don't you dare. Don't you dare come."

He watched her touch her hot, wet cleft for about ten seconds before he was ready to pounce on her. He crossed to her and thrust his fingers into her center, coating them with her slippery fragrance. She pressed against him in wanton invitation.

"Don't come," he said again as he dragged her to the couch and pushed her onto it, positioning her on her knees. "Spread your thighs and arch your back. Give me your hands." She reached back, and he took her clenched fists and held them at the small of her back as he thrust deep inside her. He reveled in the feeling of taking her, impaling her. With each stroke, each wicked slide, the stresses of the day retreated, replaced by the scent and texture of her skin. He dug his fingers into her hair, parting the strands and gripping them roughly.

"Don't you come. Don't you dare. If you do, I'll use the crop on you."

He moved his fingers around to tug on the chain attached to her clit. She gasped and went up on her toes. She rubbed her lithe body against him, and seconds later he felt her come. Rhythmic undulations and warm wetness. His balls tensed, and he felt his own climax approaching. He gritted his teeth, reaching for control.

"You naughty slut," he whispered in her ear. "You'll have to be punished now, after I'm done having my way with you."

"I'm sorry, Daniel."

"Not as sorry as you'll be when I'm cropping your ass the way you deserve."

She made a frightened moan that resonated deep in his pelvis, sending heat into raging flame. He wanted to tear her apart, fuck her to pieces. He rode her hard and fast, to the sounds of the silver chains jingling and her frantic little pants. He held her hips with a punishing grip, clenching his fingers as the wild lust inside him rose to a fever pitch. He pressed forward against her in one final joining and let the orgasm roll over him. His legs shook as hot liquid release pounded from his balls to his cock.

He caught his breath and pulled away from her. She stayed as she was, still and ready, waiting to be told what to do. He took his time just looking at her, because he never loved her more than when she was like this. Absolutely, totally in thrall to him, all animal sensation and desire. It was he who had made her that way. He liked to keep her that way for hours on end.

He wrapped his fist in her hair, breathing down her neck. "Are you ready to be punished?"

"Yes, Sir."

"Put your hands on the back of the couch, lover, and don't let go. Don't you dare move those hands."

"No, I won't."

"Hush," he said. "Just do it, no lip."

He went for the crop, rummaging around in drawers and under papers. Their stuff was scattered everywhere because they always dropped everything when they were done and crawled into bed and fucked. He found it hidden—purposely, he was sure—at the bottom of a pile of clothes and books. He came back and thwacked it hard against the arm of the couch just for effect. Those small flourishes, they really did it for her.

He made a big fuss out of positioning her properly. He pulled at her hips, cupped her spectacular, round cheeks, parted her knees even farther, and made her stick out her ass.

"You stay just like that. Be a good girl and take your punishment. I've told you a million times not to come without permission."

"I know. It's just... It's hard for me not to—"

"Are you making excuses?"

"No, Sir."

"What do I want to hear from you?"

"I'm sorry. I'm sorry, Sir."

"Not as sorry as you will be."

"Yes, Daniel," she said. Then, "Ow!" as he landed the first stroke.

He had to hand it to her. He never could have taken the pain that she did, which was why he was the Dominant and she the submissive. She trembled and cried penitent tears, but she never broke the pose. She kept her ass high in the air, offered to him for punishment. He only gave her twenty, which he made her count, and he only aimed for the plug a few times. He whacked her hard at the end, and the resulting jumps and wails were gorgeous. When he put down the crop, he reached around to take off the nipple clamps and the clamp biting between her legs. She sniffled and looked back at him with her wide blue eyes. Her distress and vulnerability triggered a delicious pang of tightness in his pelvis. He brushed back her hair and dried the few remaining tears by running his tongue lightly across her cheeks.

"Good girl," he said. "I love you."

"I love you, too."

"Let's go to dinner. I'm hungry. I'll fuck your ass when we get back."

Dominance 101: the longer you make them wait for it, the wilder they get. Another good hour and a half with that plug in her ass, reminding her of what was coming later... Nice. He could see her turning the thought of it over in her brain. *Oh no. Oh yes. But oh no.*

At the restaurant, they found a private corner table where she could sit beside him and squirm at will. "I love you," he said as he scanned the menu. "Now sit still before I bend you over this table."

"You wouldn't," she said softly.

"Are you sure of that?" Of course he wouldn't, but it was fun to pretend once in a while. "I'm already hard for you," he said, putting down the menu, "but we're going to eat first. Hmm. Just think how riled up I'll be when I finally have my go at your asshole."

She clenched her hands in her lap, and blushed as the waiter arrived. He wondered if the waiter had heard. Even if he hadn't, how could he look at Wednesday and not know she was hornier than hell? That she'd been beaten and fucked and toyed with mercilessly, and now was being made to wait over a leisurely dinner for Daniel to finish her off with his cock up her ass?

The waiter looked at him while he placed their orders, and no, the waiter didn't know. He didn't have the slightest clue. After he left, Daniel looked back at Wednesday, who was still blushing, still squirming under his gaze.

"Hanging in there, Wed?"

"I'm doing fine," she said with a smile.

But her expression said, *I want you to fuck me. Soon.*

* * *

It couldn't have been soon enough for either of them. When they returned to their room, he stopped her right inside the door and pushed her to the floor, and she moaned as he knelt behind her, pushing up her dress. He pulled out the toy and positioned his cock against her hole, then pressed into her ass slowly, into the hot, clenching channel. He took time after the long buildup to savor the moment, and gave her adequate time to adjust to his girth. He hovered over her, trying to leash the animal impulses that had him wanting to conquer, to rut. As unforgiving as steel, he held her hands above her head.

"Daniel," she said. "More..."

"Hush. I don't want to hurt you."

"I want you to hurt me."

"I know," he said, pulling her hair, "because you're a hopeless pain slut."

"Yes, Sir," she moaned, agreeing with him so wholeheartedly that he had to laugh.

"You just lie still and let me fuck you, and I'll hurt you as much as I see fit."

He pressed deeper then, with excruciating slowness, until he was all the way in. She groaned and squirmed, his horny sex toy. Each movement was bliss, a tug and tease to his throbbing cock. He ignored her restless squiggling, ignored the fact that his pants were still in a heap down by his knees. He focused on his needs for the moment, the amazing tightness of plumbing her asshole.

"Daniel!" she cried. "Please fuck me hard. Take me harder."

"Shh. Enough. I don't want to fuck you hard. I want to fuck you slow, fuck you forever. I'm going to take my time. I'm not even sure I want you to come. I think I might just use you and put you to bed unsatisfied. I always say I'll do that, but I never do." He slid in again and out, chuckling at the way her shoulders tensed. "I think it would be an edifying lesson for you. Your Dominant's needs come first. Always."

She exploded in a whine and tried to squirm away. He slapped her flank with a sharp crack.

"Stop. Ass up. Let me fuck you."

He plowed in and out, each stroke an impossible slide of excruciating pressure. He was impassioned; he was tender. He tried to make it last, but it was hard when every movement he made sent wild sparks of heat along his nerves. When he was nearly to the point of capitulation, he pressed down on her shoulders and slid deeper, then deeper still. He teetered on the cusp of a gathering cloudburst, a storm about to break wide. She twitched her bottom and buried her face in her hands. Poor, poor subbie. Orgasm denied.

"Daniel...Sir?" Her muffled voice was plaintive. "Did you really mean it? About not letting me come?"

"Yes, I really meant it. I'm not letting you come this time. Your orgasms are mine to control, yes? That's what we agreed the first day."

Another sigh. "Yes, Sir." As if resigned to her fate, she drew her legs under her, offering her bottom, giving herself up for his use. The unselfish, submissive action hit him like a lightning bolt. Hot excitement rolled over him in a crippling wave that arced up his chest and down to his cock and balls. He took her ass cheeks in his hands and pounded into her. He finished with a pulsing crescendo, an emptying of his cock that went on and on. He filled her ass with his cum, feeling powerful and totally replete.

She didn't move. He slid his fingertips down to knead her bottom, then slid them up to toy aimlessly with the neat silk hem of her dress.

"What a good girl you are. I'm so proud of you. Did you like giving up your orgasm for my pleasure?"

She was quiet, then looked back at him and answered honestly, "No, Sir. I didn't like it."

"But you did it anyway, didn't you? For me. Because I wanted it."

She buried her face in the floor. "Yes, Sir."

"Wait there. Don't move an inch." He left to clean himself up, half expecting to find her masturbating against the floor when he returned. But she was still. Beautiful obedience.

"Turn over," he said. "Lie on your back. Keep your legs parted."

She did as he asked. He surveyed his lovely girl, noted the glistening wetness of her slit and her swollen, unsatisfied clitoris. He looked at his watch, then back down at her.

"You have exactly two minutes to make yourself come. You can only use one hand. If you don't manage it, you won't get another chance until morning. Go."

She looked a bit embarrassed, but her horniness won over that. She slid her right hand down to her clit, and rubbed and touched it, arching her back. She bit her lip, her breath coming faster almost at once. Her eyes closed in erotic concentration.

"Open your eyes. Look at me."

She let out her breath in a desperate gust, but she obeyed him.

"One minute and thirty seconds left," he said, glancing at his watch.

She made a small keening sound, her eyes locked on his. She moved her fingers faster and faster with desperate abandon. She jerked her hips, and the wetness of her juices gleamed on her delicate fingers. She held his gaze until the orgasm came on her, then she closed them, lost in her own world.

But it was enough, enough to satisfy him. For the moment. Her wanton display actually had his cock twitching again. He looked down at his watch.

"Not bad. One minute and thirty seconds." He smiled at her.

She opened her eyes wide. "Still thirty seconds left? Can I try to come again?"

* * *

As the production dragged on, long days on set became a problem. Too often, Wednesday seemed bored and alone. Daniel urged her to start writing again to pass the time, and even bought her a laptop and notebooks and every type of pen. She did eventually begin to put some words on paper, after some nudging on his part and, yes, threats of punishment unless she did as he asked. But she'd still been tired and grouchy of late.

On top of Wednesday's moods, Daniel was dealing with Vincent's escalating requests for news and information. Vincent had been happy to hear she was writing again, a talent he'd always worried he had derailed with his attentions. He actually asked if Daniel would e-mail him some of her work.

"Absolutely not," Daniel had said. She wouldn't even let *him* look at it, not that he would have admitted that to Vincent. In most other things, she had grown less secretive around him, and intimacy scared her less. But her writing remained strictly off-limits. "You can look at it when it's done, Daniel." But apparently nothing was ever done, because she never showed him a thing.

Then March twenty-ninth rolled around, Wednesday's birthday. Daniel couldn't help but recall that night a year earlier—the night Vincent had shared her with him. Daniel was determined not to let those memories intrude on her birthday celebration. But when he arrived at the hotel with her favorite Thai takeout and a confection of a birthday cake, he was alarmed to find Wednesday sprawled listlessly on the couch.

He put the food down and went to kneel by her. Her color was awful, pale and greenish. Her eyes looked bloodshot like she'd been crying. He touched her forehead. "Are you sick?"

She shook her head. "I'm just tired."

Are you thinking about Vincent, and last year? He doesn't matter anymore. Just smile for me, baby. "I brought your favorite. Pork and noodles."

She put a hand to her mouth and pushed past him, then shut herself in the bathroom. He heard her being sick, then water running and audible sobbing.

He knocked on the door. "You okay in there?"

"No."

"Not the best way to spend your birthday, huh? Can I come in?"

When she didn't answer, he opened the door to find her huddled against the bathtub, her expression bleak. "Poor baby. I won't mention food again, I promise. Not until you're feeling better. The cake will keep."

"It won't keep," she said. "I'll never be feeling better."

"It's probably just some twenty-four-hour bug."

"My period is three weeks late, Daniel. And I don't think it's coming anytime soo—"

She heaved and dived for the bowl. Daniel stood, too shocked to reply or help her. *Three weeks late?* When nothing came up, she spit in the toilet and then leaned back, fixing him with a virulent look. "I told you I forgot a pill."

".Jesus, Wednesday." He was still processing the missed-period thing. "Forgot a pill? What?"

"I missed a pill, damn it! Remember? And you said not to worry about it. 'Oh, it's just one. Nothing's going to happen.' Well, I think something happened."

She started to cry again, miserable tears. It finally occurred to him to go to her. He huddled beside her on the floor and pulled her resisting form against him. "I'm sorry. I didn't think one pill would matter. But, I mean, are you sure? Have you taken a test?"

"I don't want to take a test." She pouted, wiping away tears.

He wanted to commiserate, but some frisson of curiosity started to infiltrate his brain. A little child—his and Wednesday's. What would that be like? He found the idea didn't upset him that much. "Listen, baby—"

"Don't call me baby," she snapped. "I don't want to think about babies."

"Okay, but don't overreact here. If you're pregnant, we'll deal with it. It's not the end of the world."

"It *is* the end of the world." She gazed up at him with swollen, red-rimmed eyes. "My mother died having me. She was too small. And my dad always said I was built like her, so I think..." She wrapped her arms around her waist, looking down at herself in horror. "I know I'm too small, too."

"Oh, Wednesday. Just because your mother died doesn't mean you will," he said gently. "Obstetrics as a science has come a long way. They're a lot more careful now with all the lawsuits and whatnot. Besides, there's no way I'll let you die."

"I'm sure my father felt the same way about my mother." That shut him up for a minute. Had her father always been cold and distant, or only after his wife died? Only after she'd died trying to give birth to Wednesday, the child he'd never seemed able to love?

He brushed her hair back from her tearful eyes. "I won't let anything happen to you. Believe me. Everything will be fine."

Daniel didn't believe for a second that she was going to die, or he would have ripped their baby from her womb himself. When praying fervently to lose the baby naturally didn't work for her, she made an appointment to have an abortion, which got rather involved since they were in Australia. In this, for once, he did not feel he had the authority to control her, so he held his silence and waited for the day. As he'd suspected, she was unable to go through with it and came home from the appointment a mess. She cried for hours in his arms, wretched and scared.

But from that emotional afternoon, it was a reality. They were having a baby. Wednesday and he had created a life together, however accidentally, and they would soon be a family. Shortly after they returned to Los Angeles, he made Wednesday his wife. She only fought him a little. A few good, strict spankings and a marvelous ring did the trick.

And yes, it galled him that he was doing exactly as Vincent had directed, doing exactly, to the letter, what Vincent had prescribed. *I want you to love her and baby her and discipline her and marry her and get her pregnant with little Daniels and Wednesdays.*

Vincent had been excited to hear about the baby, but he hadn't been invited to the wedding. Not a chance. Their shotgun wedding was a private affair between them and a justice of the peace. Afterward Daniel took her home and fucked her in the middle of the living room with her wedding dress over her head, and then tied her to the tree and spanked her. She wouldn't have had it any other way.

After that, they kept as well as they could to their usual routines, even as she grew and changed before his eyes. Her breasts—wow. Pregnancy and breasts. God's apology to men for those pregnancy hormones that made life a living hell.

He still found ways to discipline her, although inventiveness was the order of the day. No nipple clamps, because nipple stimulation could cause preterm labor. They had both almost cried over that. No hard spankings, no rough stuff, and no marks or welts when she had an appointment coming up. In the eighth month, she had to start going to the doctor weekly, and at that point they mostly gave up on the kinky play.

But he still fucked her, still lusted for her. He still bedeviled her even when she pushed him away, complaining she was a house, a blimp, crying that he couldn't possibly be attracted to her. He was attracted to her more than ever, although he could never convince her of that.

Unfortunately, she was also convinced her chances of survival were slim. She regularly fell into fits of deep despair and fearfulness. They attempted a childbirth class together. He hoped it might help her manage her anxiety, but all it did was make her more anxious, and she pulled him out of the classroom in the first hour. So finally he left her to her writing and her nervousness, and did all the things that had to be done to prepare. She wouldn't shop for clothes or pick out anything for the baby, ambivalent as she was, so he did everything, down to painting and fixing up the nursery down the hall from their room.

It was the smallest bedroom and the darkest, good for baby napping. He painted the walls—all of them. The rest of the house was as white as ever, but the baby got all the colors of the world, rainbows and trees and happy bears and a smiling sun. And pink bows and flowers, because they discovered in an awe-inspiring ultrasound that they were having a girl.

That was the closest he'd come to losing it with her during the pregnancy, that day when she wouldn't look at the screen. But he looked, and he saw, and he described it to her later in bed over her soft sobs and tears.

"Ten fingers, ten toes, two arms, two legs," he'd whispered, trying to infuse his voice with all the enthusiasm he couldn't draw from her. He wished he could pour it into her ears like his words—that enthusiasm and excitement she refused to feel. "It was all right there on the screen. You should have seen it. She was beautiful. I looked right into her face."

"Who did she look like?" she'd asked, curiosity overcoming her stubborn attempt not to care.

"Well. Skeletor, but she has some more time to grow and develop." She'd laughed then, relaxing against him. "You could see her eyes and her nose and her mouth, Wed. It was just amazing, seeing her there." After that they'd called their poor baby girl Skeletor for months. They were unable to decide on a name.

"Let's decide when we see her," Wednesday suggested. "You can pick out the name when you see her."

You can. Of course. *Because, Daniel, I'll be dead.*

12 CHAPTER TWELVE

The baby was going to kill her. Wednesday knew it. That was, if she didn't kick her to death first, or kill her from lack of sleep and lack of sex. Daniel tried, really tried, to fuck her, and he did manage somehow, but it was hard for her to enjoy it when she looked and felt like a whale.

From time to time, to torture herself, she went to the armoire in the corner of the bedroom to cry over the lingerie sets she used to be able to wear. She couldn't even fit one of her boobs in those skimpy bras, and it would have taken three or four of the garter belts to span her distended, grotesque waist. The baby must have weighed fifteen pounds by then. She'd never get her out. That was how the baby would kill her. Wednesday had killed her mother the exact same way, by being too big.

But no one took her concerns seriously. Not the doctor, not the nurses, Daniel least of all. She finally just stopped talking about it and resigned herself to the fact that she would die. He would see. He would be sorry later that he'd mocked her. He would understand and admit she was right when he was grieving over her body, and she'd be up in heaven, or more likely down in hell, saying, *I told you so.*

In the meantime, she busied herself writing, trying to put down her thoughts for Daniel before she was gone. She wrote an entire chapter for him about her childhood, revealing secrets she hadn't told him because they hurt too much. She wrote about her time with Vincent, trying to explain what she could never really explain.

And then she wrote about Daniel himself, about how beloved and wonderful he was, about how he'd changed her life. She loved him so much that that part was taking forever. Before the birth, she also planned to write about her hopes and dreams for their unborn child, who might survive even if she didn't.

Daniel loved to see her writing, even though she wouldn't let him read it. It was too personal for her to show it to him, at least while she was alive. When she was gone, he could read it, and hopefully it would sustain him until he was strong enough to get on with his life. She put it all in there, all the depth of her feelings for him. All the hope and happiness he'd given her, all the love and emotion she felt. He begged constantly to see what she was working on, especially as she typed through tears.

"It's too personal," Wednesday said, to get him off her back.

"Personal?" he scoffed. "You're nine months pregnant with my child. Let me see."

"No, but I love you. Maybe someday. When it's finished and perfect." *When I'm dead.*

"Speaking of finished," he said, "the nursery's almost painted. I should finish it up. We don't have much time left, do we?" He leaned down to kiss her huge belly.

No, we don't have much time left.

* * *

Wednesday stood by a window in the soothing autumn afternoon sun while Daniel painted upstairs. She let the unseasonable warmth seep into her sore bones. Her uterus felt tight and achy. She was at the printer, collating pages as well as she could over her massive belly.

She was finished writing the love letter she was leaving behind for her husband. Well, mostly. She hadn't been sure exactly how to wrap up everything, how to sum up all the amazing moments she and Daniel had had. It kind of trailed off at the end. *No matter what happens, no matter how miserable I am right now...*

She wished she could have finished it, but she had a feeling her time was almost up. She wanted to print a hard copy before it was too late. She was just secreting the pages of the document in the armoire upstairs when the phone rang. She lumbered down the stairs with a groan, holding her belly.

"Hello, Laurent household," she answered.

There was a momentary pause on the other end of the line, then, "Is Daniel there?"

She knew that voice as well as her own, had listened to it for five years. Had obeyed it and cowered under it and ached for it for half a decade of her life.

She took a deep breath. "Yes, he is."

Another pause. "Well then, Wednesday, put him on the line."

Not *Wednesday, how are you? What are you doing at Daniel's house?* Not *Wednesday, I hope you're okay.* No, just matter-of-fact orders to hand the phone over to Daniel. The sick part of it was, his voice made her instantly, unthinkingly obey. She might have asked, *Why are you calling here?* But no, she was already heading across the room.

"Just a minute."

Woodenly, she struggled back up the stairs. She'd thought she was over Vincent after a year and a half, but she was hurt that he'd ignored her and asked to speak to Daniel instead.

She opened the door to the nursery. God, so many colors.

"Don't come in here, babes. The fumes—" He looked at her face and fell silent. "What is it?"

She held out the phone to him like it was a snake.

"Vincent. For you."

She wasn't sure about the look he gave her then. It was frustration, anger, annoyance, guilt, but it wasn't surprise, and not seeing any surprise on his face...she wondered at that. He shepherded her out the door quickly. "Go. These fumes aren't good for the baby."

When she was out in the hall again, he slammed the door.

She stood there and listened, desperately trying to hear what was being said. She only heard a short, terse conversation, Daniel saying good-bye, then nothing. Back to the walls.

She drifted downstairs and collapsed on the couch, staring into space. She'd forgotten how it had felt with Vincent—that sense of worthlessness—and it scared her how easily that feeling came back.

She waited for Daniel to come down, to explain why Vincent had called, but he didn't, and she started imagining all kinds of things.

Maybe Vincent was sick or dying. Maybe he was moving away. Maybe he wanted Daniel to share her with him as Vincent had shared her once upon a time.

It wasn't until dinner that she accepted Daniel wasn't going to tell her on his own, so she asked him point-blank. "Why did Vincent call you today? What did you talk about?"

Daniel frowned and avoided her eyes. At first she thought he would ignore her question completely, but then he said, "It's none of your business."

Blame the pregnant hormones or the heartburn or the lack of sleep, or the annoyance of feeling like a whale, but she saw red at that moment. "Why the fuck did he call?"

"Calm down, Wednesday."

"No, I won't calm down!"

"You shouldn't be getting all excited in your condition."

"Fuck my condition. Why did he call?"

"To talk to me. That's all. Just to chat, okay?"

"Why? What on earth could you possibly chat about with him?"

He made a face.

"What do you have to discuss with Vincent?"

He sighed heavily. "You. Okay? You. He calls to talk about you."

She blinked at him. "He *calls*? He's called before?"

"He calls me a lot, actually."

What? Her heart rate accelerated, along with her temper. "You never told me. You never once told me he called."

"The reason for that, Wednesday, is that I didn't want you to know."

"You didn't think I had a right to know?"

"No, I didn't and I don't. I can decide not to tell you whatever I fucking please."

"Oh, that's right." She picked angrily at the food on her plate. "I'm only your fucking possession, your sex toy who's not even good for that now."

He threw down his fork. "Why do you care so much about Vincent calling? Are you still in love with him? Do you want to go back to him?"

"No, I'm just wondering why—"

"Why? Why I didn't tell you? Because I hate him. I think he's an ass. You're mine now, not his. I don't want you to care if he calls or not. It's not important. Let it go."

They both sat and fumed. She didn't know why she couldn't let it drop.

"What do you tell him about me?"

He looked at her a long time, not speaking.

"What do you tell him when he calls?" she asked again.

"I tell him how you're doing," he said. "That's all, Wed."

She took a deep breath. "Why?"

"Because that's what I agreed to do."

She crossed her arms over her chest. "What you agreed to do when?"

He looked like he would have given anything not to answer, but he did.

"When he broke up with you, so that you could start dating me." He sighed again, another great exhalation. "Okay, are you happy? What else do you want to know? Ask me everything, damn it, because I don't ever want to discuss this again."

"So you... So he..."

"He broke up with you to give you to me. In return, I agreed to keep him informed about you."

"*Informed?*"

"It's not what it sounds like. It's not nearly as bad as it sounds—"

"Isn't it? The two of you wheeled and dealed for me?"

"No! I never—"

"You bought me from him for the price of these phone calls?"

"No!"

"What do you tell him? What did you agree to tell him? The stuff we do together?"

"No, only...how you're doing. If you're happy. If you're healthy. He just wanted to keep track of how you are."

"Keep track, huh? That's lovely. Why didn't you two just go ahead and keep sharing me? Isn't that what you're doing anyway?"

"Wednesday—"

"You give him reports on me? Regularly?"

"It's not like that. Wed, come on. Don't freak out. He misses you. He's happy you're happy. Why are you so mad?"

When he reached for her, she stood and backed away. "All this time I thought I was free of him, that I had left him behind. All this time he's been more in control of me than ever. He's controlled everything. All of this!"

"I control you, Wed. Not him."

"He controlled you," she said, bursting into tears. "He talked you into taking me."

"No!" He stood and came at her then. "No, you have no idea—he didn't talk me into anything—"

"That night you came over," she sobbed. "It was an audition, wasn't it? A fucking audition."

"Stop! You get ahold of your mouth. You calm down and think about what you're saying."

"Vincent set up all of this. Our great love..."

"No, he didn't. No."

"You don't know him. You don't know how he is! You don't know how he gets off on this—controlling me, controlling you, controlling everything—"

"Yes, I do! I do know, Wednesday. Believe me, I know, but I went along with it for you, so I could have you, so he would break up with you and let you come to me."

She buried her head in her hands. "Everything, all of it, a setup."

"No. I took you because I wanted you, not because Vincent wanted me to. I watched you from the café across from your work for weeks."

"What are you talking about?"

"Vincent approached me about taking you on, but it was after! Long after I'd fallen for you."

She took a step back, her hands in fists. What was he talking about? "Long after? When did you—"

"When did I fall in love with you? The first minute we met. The first second. I fell in love with you the night of March twenty-ninth. When did I strike up a deal with him for you? Ten days later. I would have done anything to have you. I still would. I always will."

He reached for her, but she backed away again. She was almost to the damn birch tree.

"Look, sit down, baby. It's not good for you to get all excited in your condition."

"My condition," she said with derision. "Did Vincent tell you to knock me up?"

Daniel rubbed his eyes. "If you keep saying that—that I knocked you up—so help me, Wednesday."

"Well, you did!"

"You're the one who forgot to take the fucking pill! I don't think Vincent had anything to do with that."

"And you're the one who wouldn't wait! Who wouldn't go back to using condoms even though I told you I'd missed a dose."

He made a growling sound that scared her. "I swear to God, if you don't—Jesus. You're having a fucking baby." He waved his arms at her belly. "Just face facts. Get over it! Jesus. Enough. You know what would be so fucking wonderful? If you could find some fucking tiny shred of maternal instinct buried somewhere inside that messed-up brain of yours and stop whining every hour of every day about how miserable you are, how much you hate our child—"

"I don't hate our child."

"You hate her. And lately, I think you hate me. What happened to us? What happened to what we had? Was it all an act? Have you ever really loved me? I'll never be good enough for you, will I? I'll never beat you hard enough or treat you shitty enough to live up to him."

Him. The interloper in their marriage.

Wednesday was finished. She walked away from Daniel, angrier than she'd been in her life. She started up to her white room, through the white house of possibilities. It seemed to her the white was more about secrecy. Hiding the truth. Words whitewashed over because they were too messy to deal with. He followed, but she stopped him halfway up the stairs.

"Daniel, don't. If you don't get away from me right now, I promise you, things will get bad. You know how bad things will get." Red words, black anger. "Just go away. Just get the fuck away from me."

She sat in her room until she heard Daniel's door slam, then she opened her door, and she left.

* * *

She walked or, rather, waddled as fast as she could manage. If Daniel had come after her, she would have fought him tooth and nail, but he didn't. She was pretty sure he hadn't heard her leave. She walked on, furious and intent. It was dark and it was late, but she dared anybody, any hapless criminal to try to mess with her. She walked several blocks until her belly started to cramp from the strain, then hailed a cab to take her the rest of the way.

At Vincent's, she pounded on the door. When he opened it, his eyes went wide.

"Wednesday," he said in his usual placid, fuck-you tone, "what a surprise." He looked her pregnant body up and down and muttered, "You're looking...well."

She slapped his face so hard that her hand smarted. "I need to talk to you."

He rubbed his jaw and nodded. "All right. Come in."

She stood in the middle of his living room. Vincent kept his distance. "You're welcome to talk to me, Wednesday, but I won't let you hit me again."

"Okay, I'll try not to."

The submissive kneeling beside the couch stared at Wednesday as if she had two heads. Vincent waved the girl away. "Into the bedroom, Gretchen. Wait on your knees for me."

Wait on your knees, Wednesday. She'd heard it a thousand times.

"Now," Vincent said. "To what do I owe the pleasure of this visit?"

She refused to be baited by his tone. She glared at him. "Why won't you let me go?"

He looked back at her, the picture of confusion. "I don't know what you're talking about. I let you go a long time ago. Over a year ago."

"You're a liar."

He sighed. "Sit down. You look tired. Can I get you something? Some water? Tea?"

No, she wouldn't sit down, but she was thirsty as hell. She heard herself say, "Water, please," even as she decided she wouldn't take a thing from him. When she accepted the glass, she stared at his hand. She remembered it still, those long, powerful fingers, that dusting of dark hair.

He sat on the couch and leaned back, regarding her as if she was the most annoying intrusion of his life. "So, what did he tell you?"

"He said you gave me to him. Is that true?"

He considered her for a minute. "Yes, I suppose it is. Why does that bother you? You were mine to give."

Tears sprang to her eyes at the emotionless way he said that. "And in return you made him agree to report on me. To tell you about me and him."

"I just wanted to know what became of you." He shrugged. "How silly of you to be angry about it. An informal agreement between

Dominants. That's all. These types of arrangements are engineered all the time in our world. You know that."

These types of arrangements. So that was all she was. "If that's what you were doing when you released me, why didn't you warn me? Why didn't you tell me?"

"Because I do what I want, and what I do is none of your concern. Wednesday, what's become of you? What's become of my well-trained girl? All these questions—there's not an ounce of submission in you. Does he like you this way?"

"He likes me just fine. He's a better Master to me than you were, a thousand times better."

"I know. I chose him especially for you. I knew he would be good for you, be what you needed. I told him to have babies with you." He looked meaningfully at her belly. "Boy or girl?"

So Vincent had ordered the baby, too. "None of your business."

"He's apparently let you run wild. A shame. You were a great submissive once. Very good at what you did."

"I still am!" She hated how she sounded, like a child on the playground. *I'm not, you are!* "I still am a great submissive, and he's a great Dominant, and he loves me very much."

"Yes, you're welcome. You have me to thank for all this love and happiness." He said *love and happiness* like they were something dirty. "It's what I always wanted for you."

Oh, she was supposed to be grateful. "I don't like it that you gave me to him. It wasn't your right! To just give me to him like I was some cast-off thing of yours—"

"Cast-off thing?" He came off the couch, advancing on her. "I gave you like a gift. I valued you very much. I always cared for you deeply."

"Did you love me, Vincent?" she asked. "Did you ever love me?"

"Wednesday—"

"Did you? Just tell me. In five years, did you ever for a second love me?"

He was close to her now, an arm's length away. "What do you think? Did I love you? Wednesday." He looked in her eyes. "Could I have given you up any other way?"

They looked at each other eye to eye, not as submissive and Dominant, but as old, old friends. No, not friends. Lovers. Lovers who'd shared a very strange love.

"Why are you doing this?" she asked through tears. "Why won't you just let me go?"

"I'll never let you go. I can't. I can't let go of you."

"Then at least, at least..." She sniffled, wiping her nose on her sleeve. "Admit you love me, then. Just once."

He took her in his arms, slowly gathered her to him. She let him hold her tight against his chest, as tightly as her huge belly would allow. Her tears fell on his shirt. She could feel his heart beating slowly against her ear.

"Can't you say it just one time for me?" she whispered.

"Why do I have to say it when you know? But if you want me to say it, I will. I love you. I love you very much. I always will."

"But you can't have me anymore. You can't own me. You did once, but not anymore. Please, Vincent, if you love me. I'm Daniel's now."

He was quiet a long time. *Beat, beat, beat,* his heartbeat in her ear.

"Okay," he said. "I'll always love you, and you're Daniel's. Okay."

"Only Daniel's," she persisted. "I don't want to be shared."

"If you wish. Only Daniel's. Can we still be friends, though, you and I?"

"Friends?"

He held her, not loosening his hold, not until she pulled away first. She stood in front of him, suddenly weak, woozy. She was weaving on her feet. He reached for her.

"Wednesday? All right?"

Vincent had loved her. He did love her. Wasn't that all right? He had given her to Daniel because he thought it was best. Wasn't that just another form of love? Wasn't it okay? So he'd given her to Daniel. Daniel who loved her, who always had, from the moment they met. Why was that a bad thing? Why had she made it so sinister and sad?

"Vincent—" She intended to apologize, to say that yes, they could certainly be friends, that everything was okay, but then she felt a pain in her abdomen more excruciating than any she'd felt in her life. She doubled over, and if he hadn't been holding her, she would have fallen down.

"Vincent! God, it hurts! Something's wrong!"

"Nothing's wrong," he said. "This is perfectly natural. You're in labor, I think. We should probably go."

"Go? Go where?" she asked, clutching her belly.

"To the hospital. Which one?"

She started to panic. She couldn't think which hospital or what the hell to do. Vincent whipped out his cell phone and picked up her bag.

"Call Daniel," she said, a moment before she realized he already was.

"Daniel? Wednesday is with me. I think you're about to be a father." Vincent paused. She heard yelling on the other end of the line. "No, just meet us there. Which hospital is it?"

More yelling.

"I'll drive carefully, yes. We'll see you there."

By that time, Vincent had guided her to the garage and helped her into his car. She moaned in the seat next to him.

"I'm going to die, Vincent."

"You're not going to die."

"At least if I die, she'll have a good father. Not like mine."

"Your baby will have a good father," he agreed calmly. "And you'll be a good mother too. Now, enough about dying. Try to breathe through the pain."

It occurred to her that Vincent had been through this before. He had several children. Years ago, he must have driven his wife to the hospital, perhaps this same way.

"If I don't make it," she whispered, "tell Daniel I love him, and that I'm so sorry I came to see you without telling him."

"You can tell Daniel you're sorry and you love him a few minutes from now when we get to the hospital and you safely deliver your baby. And after you're recovered, I hope he punishes you very soundly for your erratic behavior tonight."

She held on to her seat hard, trying to steel herself against the pain. She felt a great rush of warmth between her legs and looked down in dread.

Blood? No, just water. Her water had broken in Vincent's car.

"It's coming. Oh God, I don't want this. I'm not ready."

"How far apart are the contractions?" Vincent asked.

"How far apart?" she repeated, dazed. Oh God, it hurt so bad.

"How long between them? Didn't you take a childbirth class or something?"

"No. Why would I? I can take pain."

"It appears you can't take pain as well as you used to."

"Shut up," she yelled so loudly that her voice cracked.

"Listen, how long have you been in labor? Contractions don't just come on like this."

"Oh, I didn't realize you were an obst-obtrec-obster—doctor."

"I'm not an obstetrician, dear, but I've been through this before. How long have you been having contractions?"

"I don't know. I've had them every day this week. A little more the last day or two. But painless ones, nothing like this."

"No, they start mildly. They only get hard and close at the end. So how far apart would you say? Ballpark."

"It's just...it's just one long contraction. I don't know."

"Well, fuck," he said. "Do not have a baby in my car. Do not. You just press those pretty little thighs together, and you wait."

Her throaty scream drowned out his stern orders. She panted as the crippling pain subsided for precious moments. Vincent made a quick call on his cell, telling Gretchen to go home, but before he even hung up, she was screaming again. She couldn't help it. It felt like the thing inside her was clawing to get out with dull, jagged razors. By the time they arrived at the ER, she was panting instructions for her funeral to Vincent. He ignored her, half helping, half carrying her inside.

"This woman is in labor," he said.

Wednesday looked around the crowded waiting room with wild eyes. *Someone, anyone, make this agony stop.* But no one turned and no one came to help them. "Jesus Christ!" Wednesday screamed, clutching her middle. "I have to lie down, now!"

That seemed to light a fire underneath them all, and someone came running with a gurney. They helped her onto it and strapped belts and monitors onto her belly. She fought with them while a nurse walked beside her, asking questions. She turned her head away, feeling hot and cold, damp with sweat. Was this what dying felt like? The nurse was persistent, snapping her fingers in Wednesday's face. "Name, age, week of pregnancy, doctor's name?" If Wednesday could have, she would have broken the woman's hand off. Vincent jumped in to answer some of the questions.

"Her name is Wednesday Carson-Laurent, and she's twenty-five years old. I don't know the name of her doctor or how pregnant she is, but she looks about done."

"Aren't you the father?"

"No, I'm just a friend, but the father will be along soon, I assure you."

The father. Daniel. Where was he? Wednesday heard his voice from somewhere far off. She could have sworn he was yelling, but she couldn't think why. "That would be him," said Vincent.

At that moment, alarms started going off and voices started speaking sharply. The gurney jerked to a stop and changed direction. She clutched at her belly, tangling her fingers in wires and stretchy belts. Faces swam above her; arms and hands pulled and prodded at her.

"What's going on?" she heard Vincent ask, but no one answered him. They ran, leaving him behind.

At least if I die... At least if I die...

She struggled and shook her head, trying to stop them from taking her. She wasn't ready to go yet. No, not so soon. She tried to scream, to ask for help, but no words came. The pain was vicious, turning her inside out. Her spine was cracking. Her teeth chattered, and she felt her gorge rising. She closed her eyes against the terrible bright lights shining down on her, undulating and fading around the edges.

She was dying. She needed Daniel. She wanted to say good-bye.

She hadn't wanted to face this alone.

13   Chapter Thirteen

The nurse blocked them both at the door. "This is a sterile area, gentlemen. Just a minute. You will have to wait here."

Just a minute.

Those words didn't compute with Daniel. Fuck, that was his wife. He watched through the window as she disappeared down the hallway. Her black curls fell down the back of the white gurney as she struggled and shook her head. He stared and stared at those curls. Oh God, she needed him. He beat on the doors, which were, of course, securely locked and accessible only with a white hospital card. He looked around for one to rip off someone's neck.

"Daniel." Vincent reached out to him.

Daniel pushed him hard against the wall. "What did you do?"

"I drove her to the hospital. That's all. I didn't do anything to her."

He couldn't believe this was happening. He couldn't believe she'd run to Vincent without telling him. He couldn't believe it was Vincent who'd driven her here. He was the father. He was her husband. No one should have taken care of her but him. No one could take care of her like he could. Now he'd had the door slammed in his face, and Vincent holding him back.

Vincent shook him and pushed him away. "Get ahold of yourself. She's going to need you soon. Calm down."

"What happened? Why is she in there?"

"The baby's in distress."

"Oh God, Wednesday was right. She's going to die. It's all my fault."

"Jesus Christ," Vincent said. "You two. She just needs an emergency C-section. It happened with my first wife. She and the baby will be perfectly fine. Why don't we go sit in the lobby and wait?"

"I'm not going anywhere. I'm waiting right here until someone lets me in. That's my *wife*."

"Yes, we all heard you yelling that earlier. I'm sure they're aware."

"Just shut up and get out of here."

Vincent leaned against the wall. "I'm not leaving until I know she's okay."

"No, you're leaving. Now. This is all your fault!"

"My fault? How so?"

"You and your stupid-ass phone call. You couldn't call my cell like every other time?"

"I tried your cell. You weren't returning my messages."

"You got her all riled up. Why didn't you hang up when she answered? You still want to be with her. You're trying to sabotage us, and guess what? It fucking worked."

"Jesus, Daniel. I play with different submissives now. Plenty of them, actually."

"None of them are like her!"

"No, they aren't. But they'll have to do, since I can't have what you have." Vincent's voice broke, a small catch of emotion that caught Daniel by surprise. He'd never seen cool Vincent lose his composure, not once.

"Why did she come to you? What did she say?"

"It's private," the older man said. "It's personal. I'd rather not share."

Daniel could easily have killed him, which probably showed in his face, because Vincent added, "Nothing inappropriate, I promise you. What do you think, that she came back to be with me? That I'd try to woo her back while she was in labor with your child? There's too much water under that bridge. Believe me, she's yours. We just came to some...understandings. It was long overdue."

"What kind of understandings?"

"Understandings you wouldn't understand. Some business between me and her, and now it's finished. It's all straightened out. Let's just say..." Vincent searched for words a moment. "I guess I confused owning her and loving her. The two ideas got tangled up in my head."

Daniel just stared. "I had to work that out too," he finally replied, remembering angry red words scrawled on white walls. "It's possible to do both, I guess. But maybe not always...the best thing to do." The door banged open then, startling both of them, and the nurse stared them down with a frown.

"One visitor only," she said. "The father can come back."

The father. That was him.

Daniel could barely put on the paper socks, the paper outfit, and the gloves fast enough. He heard the baby when he walked into the room, but all he saw was Wednesday still asleep on the table... Asleep or...? No, not dead. He could see her chest rising and falling, even though she was as pale as the grave.

"Is she okay?" Daniel asked the doctor over the crying of the baby.

"Yes, she's fine," he said. "Your wife will wake up from the anesthesia soon. In the meantime, would you like to hold your baby girl?"

Daniel nodded, staring at the bundle the nurse was holding. The woman smiled and laid the baby in his arms.

Daniel fell in love at first sight for the second time. He took in every amazing detail. Her eyes were screwed shut, her mouth was in full wail, but her hair, oh...her hair was Wednesday through and through. Blue-black, thick, and already curly. Some instinct made him start to bounce the infant, hold her close and rock her. She calmed and blinked open bleary eyes to look at him. Blue, so blue. She looked so much like her mother that he could only stare.

Wednesday started to cough and awakened with a soft moan. He handed the baby back to the nurse and went to her side.

"Wednesday." He put his head down beside hers.

She was still groggy, trying to focus on his face. "Daniel. Where's our baby?"

"Right over there. Does anything hurt? Are you all right?"

She smiled a weak smile. "I'm fine. I'm just tired. And I'm sorry..."

"Sorry for what?"

"I'm sorry I went to Vincent's. I'm sorry you weren't here. I'm sorry everything went crazy. I know you wanted to be here."

"Oh God, don't cry. Look. Look at our perfect, beautiful baby."

The nurse brought the baby over, and he and Wednesday leaned over her while he brushed back Wednesday's hair.

"Look at her, Wed. Just look at her."

"She's sleepy," she whispered as the baby yawned and sighed.

Daniel stared at his beautiful girl, the mother of his child. "You did everything perfectly, baby. You did."

"Wow." Wednesday couldn't take her eyes off the baby. "What are we going to call her? I guess now we have to come up with a name."

"Well, it's obvious, isn't it? Today's Tuesday. Tuesday, it is."

"No." She laughed. "No way. Not a chance."

"No? We could try to make a whole week together, you and me."

She rolled her eyes at that suggestion. "Seriously, Daniel. What do we call her? She looks so sweet. She looks so calm and peaceful."

He remembered that nursery rhyme again. *Tuesday's child is full of grace...*

"Hmmm. How about Grace?"

* * *

Wednesday stared and stared. Baby Grace was such a wonder. So tiny, yet so strong. So new and magical. A miracle—and best of all, they were both very much alive.

Grace looked just like Wednesday, but she wouldn't be like her. Wednesday was determined about that. She wouldn't grow up anything like her. She made that promise to her without words, over and over. A promise from the heart as she cuddled her child.

Daniel said Grace was like Wednesday because she cried all the time. Ha, very funny.

Vincent came in to see the new baby as soon as they were settled in the recovery room. Wednesday was surprised to see Vincent and Daniel being so civil with each other, but she supposed they'd had some time to talk. Vincent picked up Grace like a seasoned pro and held her close. Wednesday and Daniel looked on in shock as he cooed and dandled her in his arms.

"What?" he asked when he noticed them gawking at him. "I've done this before. In fact, I have a grandson now." He reddened slightly. "Last June."

So Master Vincent was a doting grandpa. The whole world was upside down.

"How lovely she is, Wednesday," Vincent said, sobering. "You did a really good job."

"I had something to do with it," Daniel said.

Vincent and Wednesday both scoffed.

"Yeah, you did the easy part," said Vincent. "You didn't even have to drive her here, listening to her earsplitting screams. Honestly, next time invest in some earplugs. Trust me."

Daniel chuckled, but Wednesday was too spaced-out on the strangeness of the moment to laugh. Daniel and Vincent sharing a joke while Vincent—*Vincent*—cuddled their newborn baby.

"That's a sweet child," he cooed. "Smile for Uncle Vincent. That's a good girl."

"Oh hell no, Uncle Vincent," Daniel said. "No way. You won't order this girl around."

* * *

So everything was okay between them, at least for the most part. They still had their awkward moments with Vincent, but he was part of their lives now, for better or worse.

She and Daniel took to parenting like pros, even though for a few trying months Gracie pulled them away from their erotic times together. It was hard not having that release, that intimacy for a while. But it was a small sacrifice to make for a miracle like her. When they did finally get back to it, they appreciated it that much more.

Daniel was determined that they ease back in slowly. Wednesday wanted to jump his bones willy-nilly, but of course, as always, Daniel was in charge. He tormented her terribly while she was recovering, taking things one step at a time. He loved to tie her up and tease her. *Is that what you want, you naughty little slut? Maybe next time.*

While she waited impatiently for him to play with her again the way he used to, she took care of Gracie and went back to work part-time at a new editing job, one she could do from home. Daniel pitched in whenever he could, so they both had time to work, and time together, and time to be with Grace.

It was about six months after Wednesday had given birth that they got a babysitter and went on a date. Daniel watched her from the bed while she got ready. "Stockings, Wed," he said. "No panties. Wear stockings tonight."

"Yes, Sir," she said.

It wasn't exactly like their pre-Gracie dates. They both sat at the table in the restaurant, feeling there was something they'd forgotten.

"She's fine," he said when Wednesday fell silent and thoughtful for the umpteenth time.

"I know. I know she is."

"You're such a mommy now." He said it like, *You're such a goddess.* "I knew it all along."

"Knew what?"

"That you wouldn't die. That you would love our baby girl like mad."

"I do love her," she said, "and I love you too. I love being here with you."

"I love being here with you too. God, Wed, you look beautiful tonight."

Yes. Yuck. Disgusting. They went on like that for two hours, over wine and salad and dinner and dessert, the most disgustingly loved-up conversation anyone had ever heard, and the whole time she ached for him. The way he looked at her, like he wanted to jump her—it made her so hot. By the time the waiter brought the check, Daniel was snaking his hand up her dress to follow her silk stocking to the top and touch her bare skin.

"I swear I'm going to fuck the shit out of you," he whispered. "I'm going to fuck you so hard when we get home."

When they arrived there, they threw money at the babysitter and nodded impatiently at her recap of the evening's events. *Baby's sleeping? She's fine? Okay, well, call you next time! Good-bye!*

She wanted him the second the door closed. She wanted him to push her to the floor the way he did sometimes when he just had to have it. But no. He had that gleam in his eye.

"Go to the tree, Wednesday. Go stand there."

She sighed and did as he said. He watched her for a minute, then came over and cut off one of the lower branches. He peeled the bark slowly, deliberately, eyeing her for maximum effect. When he finished, he stood close behind her and had her hold the branch while he unbuttoned her dress and pulled it over her head.

Her tummy flip-flopped with nervous lust. He was going to lay into her; she just knew it. He pressed her to the tree trunk and whispered in her ear, "Should I tie you, Wed? It's been a while. It's been a long time since you've really been disciplined."

"What am I being disciplined for?"

"I don't need a reason, do I, baby?" He pressed against her, pulling on her hair, gently at first, then hard enough to make her cry out in the silence. "Shh. Be a good girl. Answer me. Do I need a reason to hurt you?"

"No, Sir."

He closed his teeth on her earlobe, just a little bite. "God, I love you so much."

He had her wrap her arms around the tree and cuffed her hands in front so she couldn't pull them loose, then tied her around the waist. She couldn't move at all, couldn't move her ass one inch to get away as he whipped her with the switch. Switches gave a stinging, sharp pain almost as bad as a cane, and it hurt. She moaned at each stroke and tried to pull against the rope that held her, but the pain was a relief too.

It was so reassuring and wonderful. It was his way of saying, *Yes, I'll still be rough with you. Yes, you're a mother now with a baby, but I'll still treat you the same.* He beat her ass until the safe words began to turn around in her head. *Untie me, Daniel.* Then, of course, he knew that, and he stopped. He put down the switch and dropped to his knees. He rubbed and kissed the welts forming on her ass cheeks while she moaned from the combination of pleasure and pain.

"You beautiful girl. You look so punished standing there."

"I feel punished," she said, although he hadn't drawn tears. She was far too aroused to be crying. To her relief, she heard him shedding his clothes.

She waited for words, for promises of what he would do, but he only said, "Stay right there," and went into the bedroom. He returned, and she felt the cold, sticky lube against her ass and then the toy—ouch—a big one, stretching her open, then thrusting home between her burning cheeks.

"How do you feel now, Wed? Do you feel like a naughty girl? Are you afraid? But horny?"

"Yes, Sir," she managed to say, and she truly did feel all those things. She was tied quite immovably to the trunk of the tree, and now, with the massive toy in her ass, she felt more controlled and dominated than ever. The exciting part was that she passed back and forth by this tree all day, every day. Whenever she did, she remembered all the moments like these, with a hot blush and wetness between her thighs. She was sure he remembered too.

He fondled her ass for a long time while she floated on the feel of his hands. Then he sidled up behind her and fucked her. Even though she was tied there, even though she couldn't move an inch, he pushed his way inside and took possession of her in yet another way. He owned her through and through.

The muscles of his chest and stomach slid against her back, hard and unyielding. The crisp hair on his hips and chest tickled her skin, and the tree bark pricked at the front of her. His fat cock filled her, rubbing against the toy in her ass. He reached around to insinuate his large fingers between the tree and her clit, and he stroked and pinched her there until she was bursting. She was imprisoned in rope, unable to flail around with her hips the way she wanted to.

"Oh, oh...Daniel..." She came with a groan, scratching the bark as she strained at the cuffs that held her. She was filled and fulfilled. Her pussy and ass contracted around the rigid protrusions inside her, and the hot flush of completion flooded her veins. Her heart raced and her nipples scraped with delicious torment against the rough surface of the tree. When she slumped with exhaustion, he released her, and she fell into his arms, a very grateful, well-used girl.

He carried her upstairs and stripped off her shredded stockings, then tucked her into bed. "The toy will stay in your ass all night," he said, "so you can remember how much you belong to me."

"Yes, Sir," she said. "I'm yours."

14 CHAPTER FOURTEEN

Daniel was supposed to be working, but he couldn't. He kept staring over at the tree. How wonderful to have a tree in the house to tie his lovely wife to. He smiled, remembering how she'd positively hummed there the night before. The stroke of genius had been tying her around the waist. Next time he'd have to be sure to fuck her ass, maybe even use less lube than usual, so it felt a little, just a little bit, as if she were being forced. Darling pervert. God, he loved her.

She'd gone with Grace this morning to Baby Time at the library, and he was supposed to be doing some work. And he would, just as soon as he finished mooning over her. He got up a moment later and went upstairs.

He thought he might hop online and buy her another outfit. Another bra and garter belt set, or maybe a corset or some slutty dress. He went to the armoire to see what she lacked, what color, what style. He laughed to be confronted with exactly how many sets she had.

He began to sort through them, remembering this night, that night, this day, that wondrous afternoon. He looked at them all, each set wrapped in crinkly tissue, until he got to the bottom. Then he stopped, staring, because there, with his name on it, was a white envelope labeled *If I Die*...

He walked downstairs with it and sat for a long time, looking at the envelope. He was sure this was some leftover handiwork from before Grace's birth, when Wednesday had been so certain her death was imminent. She'd chosen a perfect place to hide it if she wanted to be certain he found it after her untimely demise. He would have sorted miserably through those corsets and garters, remembering in his grief all the ways he'd known her, just as he reminisced, in happiness, over them now.

He turned the envelope over in his hand. It was heavy, too heavy to just be her notes on funeral arrangements. He struggled with his conscience, about whether to open it. He thought he should wait until she returned home and ask permission. But then, it was obviously meant for him. It had his name on the front, clear as day. If it was his, why shouldn't he look inside? He ignored the fact that it said, in large black swirly letters, *If I Die*, since she most definitely hadn't died, and he wanted to open it anyway. He undid the clasp and pulled out the papers, which were, in fact, a lengthy manuscript with a letter on top.

Dear Daniel,

If you're reading this, I guess I died. I told you so. But I'm so, so sorry I've left you. That wasn't ever what I wanted to do. I wanted to be with you forever, because only with you did I feel truly loved.

OWNING WEDNESDAY

He stopped reading, already choked up with sentiment, yet chuckling at the way she wrote so matter-of-factly from beyond the grave. He had to read it all now, start to finish. He sat back on the couch, cradling the pages in his hands.

I'm sorry I wasn't more open with you, especially in the beginning. You know it was hard for me. It wasn't because I didn't love you. It was just the weight of all I had to say. But I want to say it to you now. Everything. I want you to know everything I felt, everything I wanted, everything I loved about you, and everything you always wanted to know that I couldn't express. So these pages are for you.

Please take care of our baby girl, Daniel, if she survived. When she's older, if you think it's a good idea, let her read this too, and every night, every night of her life, give her kisses from me.

I love you.

Wednesday

He thrust the note aside, as much as he loved it, adored it, to get at the manuscript. He couldn't read the words fast enough. If she arrived home and saw him reading it, he knew she would take it away.

I was born on a Wednesday...

He read with his brows furrowed and his heart in his throat. Her voice was so true, so vitally there on the page, that if she'd really died, he didn't know that he could have read it at all. It would have been like reading with her ghost right beside him. He could hear her voice, soft and sweet in his ear.

I didn't have much of a childhood, but I made it through each day.

She went on about her youth, her experiences with her father, which were very hard to read. It was so bleak a story he was actually relieved when Vincent came into the picture. She spoke of him, also, matter-of-factly, just telling the story and not the deeper feelings, perhaps to protect Daniel. Or perhaps she still didn't believe in her heart that Vincent loved her as much as he did, that she was worthy of that love Vincent held for her, like a secret, deep in his heart.

From Vincent, the story moved on to meeting him. He smiled and bit his lip, reading over her account of how she'd felt when they met. He was so touched at the carefully chosen words, each carrying so much weight. He had to say she'd nailed it exactly, every pang, every secret thrill he'd also felt. She went on to describe her love for him, her most heartfelt feelings, in such depth and detail that he could hardly bear it.

She could never have said such things to his face. He knew that. That was just the way she was. But it was a gift of untold value to finally hear the things she felt. He was so captivated, so moved by her writing that he didn't hear her come in. She found him there when he was at the end, where it abruptly cut off midsentence, during the abject misery of her ninth month of pregnancy. *No matter what happens, no matter how miserable I am right now...* Then it stopped.

He looked up at her, and he would have felt guilty if he hadn't been so overwhelmed with emotion. She didn't look mad or embarrassed. She mostly looked like she wanted to run.

"You weren't supposed to find that. I forgot I'd hidden it there."

"I found it," he said. "I read it all, until the end. Come here." His voice was thick with emotion. "Come here to me right now."

She left Gracie sleeping in her baby seat and walked over to him. He put the manuscript down with an effort. He wouldn't let her take it away from him, that was for sure. He would have fought her tooth and nail before he'd let her take it away.

"Are you mad that I read it?" he asked.

"Are you mad at me?"

"No. Why would I be?" He gathered her in his arms and brushed her hair back. She wouldn't look at him.

"I should have told you all those things. I wish I could have. But I couldn't."

"It's okay, I know. I knew them anyway. I felt them in my heart. But your writing, Wednesday, it's so beautiful. I had no idea you had all those words inside."

She looked thoughtful then, as if she was remembering something, but she stayed silent. He reached down to pick up the manuscript and showed her the last page. "But the end here—you didn't finish."

She looked sheepish. "I tried to finish it a few times, but I couldn't. I just couldn't find the words." She sniffled, growing calm. "I couldn't find any words that were big enough and deep enough to sum up what we had."

"What we *have*," he said, wiping away the single tear that rolled down her cheek. "I still have you, and you still have me. I have you forever, Wednesday, and we don't need any words for that."

* * *

Long ago, or it seemed like long ago anyway, she had knelt at Vincent's feet. She'd been bursting with words, reeling from the pain of keeping them inside.

Daniel had said to her, "I had no idea you had all those words inside." But she didn't, not anymore, because with Daniel, those trapped words finally found voice. Not in any one story or any one conversation, but over days, over weeks, over a lifetime of moments in two years. How could she possibly have distilled all that life and love Daniel had shown her into something as workaday as words? It would have been an impossible task, and she realized now she had been foolish to try.

No, it wasn't words that could define her and Daniel. It wasn't words that would make sense of their lives and the strange, intense love they felt for each other. No, it was moments, those moments he gave her like magic. Moments like a pot full of gold at the end of a rainbow, each glittering disk infused with its own priceless story. Moments like stars in the sky, impossible to quantify or understand, but magnificent all the same. There were so many of them, each a droplet in a waterfall, and they poured on her whenever she needed to remember she was loved.

"I'd like to have her alone."

"What do you want, Wednesday? Where do you want to go next in life?"

"Well, you know why it hurts, don't you, Wednesday? Why I hurt you?"

"You were made to wear white, a sweet girl like you."

"I do own you. That's not in question. You're mine like water is wet."

"I won't let anything happen to you. Believe me."

"Stockings, Wed. Wear stockings tonight."

"You're such a mommy now. I knew it all along."

"Do you understand me, Wednesday Carson?"

Yes, she understood. She understood everything deeply, elementally, although she could never have put it all to words. She finally realized what really mattered—that Daniel loved her, and that she was, as he'd always insisted, worthy of that love.

Later, Wednesday drifted in thoughts of him. She was secured to his bed by soft white restraints. He knelt over her, taking his time. He ran his fingers up to the tops of her white stockings, then down to her ankles, avoiding her ticklish spots. Every few seconds he looked into her eyes, a deep gaze of fondness. She found herself blushing under his scrutiny. *Oh, Wednesday, really?* She hadn't thought she still retained the capacity to feel embarrassment.

He parted her with his fingers, moving with slow and gentle deliberation. Her gaze was riveted on his lips, the way they parted and then pursed in concentration as he touched her. She wrapped her hands around the restraints and held tight as he leaned to drop teasing kisses down her belly, over her white garter belt, and to the pale scar just above the apex of her mons.

She twisted, feeling the tickle of soft lace as he slid his tongue between the lips of her sex and blazed a path of delicate torment right down to her very center. She jerked her hips as he flicked his tongue in and out of her. *Yes yes yes.* He twisted his fingers around her elastic garters and licked from one edge of her cleft to the other, then nipped lazily at her clit, a delicious, concentrated ache. Her pelvis throbbed with building arousal. "Oh God, Daniel, please."

His mouth left her, and she moaned helplessly. He kissed up her belly again, then over to her hard nipples and the curves of her shoulders. She turned her head to kiss him back, feeling his light stubble brushing against her cheek. She licked behind his ear and drifted on the fresh, heady scent of him. She was acutely aware of the heat of his cock lying heavily against her thigh. When she moaned, he took her head in his hands and kissed her mouth, a long, lingering kiss of heat and secret, urgent breaths. He caressed her nipples at the same time. Then he pinched them, stirring the fire into a frenzy.

"Please," she begged in a whisper against his lips.

"In a minute. When I want."

His control was epic while hers was nonexistent, but she tried like a good girl to please him. She tried to behave and not plead for satisfaction as he dipped inside her just a little, then out, then in again. She moaned as softly as she could, but it was impossible for those sighs and moans not to escape.

"Quiet. Shh." He silenced her with one light finger against her lips. "I'm going to fuck you. And you can come, Wednesday, as many times as you like, for being a good girl, such a very good girl to me today."

He spoke about the letter he'd found, the long letter she'd written for him, that had made his eyes glaze over with emotion and love and things she couldn't grasp. Had she wanted him to find it there at the bottom of the armoire, under all those stockings and garters? She'd left it there even though she hadn't died, and let herself believe she'd only forgotten. But deep inside she knew she'd wanted him to find it. She'd needed him to know all the things she couldn't say.

Now he knew. Yes, that much was obvious. She could tell just from the way he came inside her, grasping her close as if he were one with her. He ran his fingers over her, everywhere. Suddenly she wanted to do the same. She wanted, more than anything, to hold him close too, to touch his soft, unruly hair, the mat of fur on his chest, his muscular, powerful buttocks as he thrust inside her, making her his again and again.

She was his, completely and without question. He owned her as much as he owned himself, their daughter Gracie, and his white house of possibilities, with the strange tree that grew from the center of it. He owned all of it, and his ownership was absolute.

To be fair, they owned him too—she and Gracie. He was theirs every bit as much as they were his. Wednesday needed him to release her just for a moment, to undo those velvet cuffs that held her in his power, so she could touch him as he was touching her.

"Untie me, Daniel," she said. He stopped midthrust and looked down at her.

"What hurts? What's wrong?"

"I'm not safe-wording. I just need you to unbind me. I need to hold you. I want to touch you. Please!" Her voice grew stronger with each word. "I want to put my hands on you. Please, let me go. Untie me, Daniel."

Rrrrip. Rrrrip. With an indulgent smile, he released her. She pulled him close and wrapped her arms tightly around his neck.

"Better?" he whispered in her ear.

"Better," she said with a sigh, and after that there was no more need for words.

He cupped her bottom, holding her close as he fucked her, as if there was no possible way to get as close as he wanted. She just held him tight and put her trust in him, because she knew, with his arms always around her, she would be safe. He had taught her about care, and he had taught her about love. He had taught her about possibilities...

"God, Wednesday," Daniel said against her cheek. "I love you in white."

You may also enjoy

these BDSM romances by Annabel Joseph

The award-winning Rough Love series

There's rough sex, and then there's rough love. The challenge is learning the difference...

Chere's a high-class call girl trapped in a self-destructive spiral, and "W" is the mysterious and sexually voracious client who refuses to tell her his name. Over the span of four years, their tortured relationship unwinds by fits and starts, encompassing fear and loneliness, mistrust, aggression, literal and figurative bondage, and moments of excruciating pain.

But there's also caring and longing, and heartfelt poetry. There are two deeply damaged people straining to connect despite the daunting emotional risks. When he slaps her face or grasps her neck, it's not to hurt, but to hold. His rough passions are a plea, and Chere's the only one so far who's been able to understand...

The Rough Love series is:
#1 Torment Me
(Winner—BDSM Writers Con Best Dark Erotica Novel—2016)
#2 Taunt Me
#3 Trust Me

The BDSM Ballet series

Waking Kiss... A stranger in the wings, a traitorous pair of toe shoes, and a traumatic turn dancing with The Great Rubio... For ballerina Ashleigh Keaton, it's been one hell of a night.

But it's not over yet. When Rubio drags her to a private party at his friend's house in the ritzy part of London, she meets Liam Wilder, a lifestyle dominant and frighteningly seductive man. Liam pursues Ashleigh, attracted by her strength and talent, but she has secrets — an abusive past and a crippling fear of intimacy that prevents her from connecting to anyone, especially a playboy reputed to be legendary in bed. How pure are his motives? Is he helping her or endangering her fragile soul?

Fever Dream... Petra Hewitt's the top ballerina in the world, and The Great Rubio her obvious counterpart, so why does she want to strangle him whenever he's around? He's haughty, abrupt, demanding — and alarmingly sexy. Petra knows Rubio is dangerous to her heart, to her peace of mind, and worst of all, to her career, but his rough flirtation compels her. When she gets a chance to play with him at a BDSM party, their professional partnership takes a feverish left turn.

But as they enjoy their sensual games of dominance and submission, career pressures mount, and an overzealous fan brings dangerous tension to their relationship. Soon, the dream gives way to the stark reality of her vulnerability. Maybe, just maybe, some risks are too terrifying to take.

The Comfort series

Have you ever wondered what goes on in the bedrooms of Hollywood's biggest heartthrobs? In the case of Jeremy Gray, the reality is far more depraved than anyone realizes. Brutal desires, shocking secrets, and a D/s relationship (with a hired submissive "girlfriend") that's based on a contract rather than love. It's just the beginning of a four-book saga following Jeremy and his Hollywood friends as they seek comfort in fake, manufactured relationships. Born of necessity—and public relations—these attachments come to feel more and more real. What does it take to live day-to-day with an A-list celebrity? Patience, fortitude, and a whole lot of heart. Oh, and a *very* good pain tolerance for kinky mayhem.

The Comfort series is:
#1 *Comfort Object* (Jeremy's story)
#2 *Caressa's Knees* (Kyle's story)
#3 *Odalisque* (Kai's story)
#4 *Command Performance* (Mason's story)

ABOUT THE AUTHOR

Annabel Joseph is a NYT and USA Today Bestselling BDSM romance author. She writes mainly contemporary romance, although she has been known to dabble in the medieval and Regency eras. She is known for writing emotionally intense BDSM storylines, and strives to create characters that seem real—even flawed—so readers are better able to relate to them. Annabel also writes non-BDSM romance under the pen name Molly Joseph.

You can follow Annabel on Twitter (@annabeljoseph) or Facebook (facebook.com/annabeljosephnovels), or sign up for her mailing list at annabeljoseph.com.